ROMANCING THE GALAXY

ADVENTURES OF A COSMIC WANDERER

Luckey K.D.

First edition

ISBN: 979-8-9910319-6-7

*This book was professionally typeset on Reedsy.
Find out more at reedsy.com*

*"For the days I felt invisible, for the nights I wished I was.
For the war inside me that no one saw and the battles I lost in
silence. If nothing else, this book proves that I existed,
even if only in the margins of the universe."*

Contents

Acknowledgments

This book wasn't written alone, even if it felt like it. To those who stood by me, who reminded me why I started—thank you. To those who doubted me, who walked away—thank you too. You fueled something in me I didn't know I had.

But at the end of the day, I don't owe this book to anyone but myself. I wrote this in the quiet hours, in the moments no one saw, with nothing but my own thoughts and will to keep me going. This is my proof that I can create something out of nothing.

And that's enough."

Chapter 1

Heartbreak

You recognize a person at their worst or their best... Do you choose to deal with a person based on their worst, or their best? How should you decide?

Herein lies the irony, thought Noir, sitting across from her. Those who choose one way or the other move forward with their life. Those who cannot decide are trapped in the illusion, some force beyond the comprehension of the human mind. It was not his intention to sigh, yet one escaped without his permission.

She caught it. His heart sank seeing her eyes narrow. *"What? Am I boring you?"*

Noir's mind went blank. How does one respond to that? There were no lines on her flawless face except for the few unsettling ones between her brows. It was hard for him to grasp how someone he had once loved so deeply could look at him like that. The cold, unfeeling gaze in her eyes felt like falling into the void of space without a spacesuit— chilling to the bone, suffocating. *"No,"* he barely whispered, and somehow, that was all he could say.

Her eyes drifted away as if his gaze was too much to bear. Fortunately, the waitress arrived. Noir felt uneasy in her presence; something held him back from looking up and meeting her eyes. But she was quite professional, and she was especially kind to him as she took their orders, if Noir hadn't imagined it.

Even that didn't seem to escape Madison's notice, and a flicker of quiet fury appeared in the iris of her eyes for a moment. Their food arrived shortly, and they began to eat.

Dinner tables are for conversation, for bonding, not just for eating. Those present should converse. But Noir found nothing to say, recalling all the times words flowed between them so easily, like two friends reconnecting after a long time, with hours passing in laughter and idle chatter. It had been like that every day with her, then it stopped… "So, how was your day?" he said, merely to break the silence, uttering the most clichéd thing imaginable.

"Working, that's how," she answered, and he wished he'd let the silence linger. *"Stupid Lawson lost three hours of data I submitted. How the hell do you lose that? You have to be the most bumbling, inept, foolish idiot in the entire universe!"*

Noir made a sympathetic expression and asked sweetly, *"That's terrible. What did you do?"*

"I had to redo everything! Do you know what it's like to repeat a mind-numbing task? It feels like chewing on a ball of someone else's hair that you found in the drain, but for three hours!" She stabbed her meat with a fork, tore off a piece, and began chewing on it. *"What about you?"*

Noir quietly set down his fork and knife; his appetite had vanished. Crossing his arms, he leaned forward over his plate. Taking a breath, he said, *"Well, good news—I got another job."*

Madison swallowed, not just her food but also the words that had clearly formed at the tip of her tongue. Instead, she asked, *"Where is it?"*

"Oh, it's not that far," Noir said, gesturing toward the window as if the destination lay just beyond its frame. *"It's over in the OB region. The Eorr planet. I think I can visit you twice a month."*

Madison forced a smile. *"What kind of job is it?"*

"Well, I'm not exactly sure," Noir shifted in his seat. *"I accepted right away because this job is going to last a while. And the client seemed legitimate, too. From a reputable government. They've always paid their contractors well."*

"I'm happy for you," she said, though her voice lacked any warmth.

"What?"

"It's nothing, I told you. Congratulations!"

"Oh, come on, Maddie, don't be like that—"

"I just don't understand why you would choose that unstable, crappy work over a real job!" Madison snapped. *"I went out of my way to find you that perfect, respectable job, and you threw it away for this?"*

"I know, and I appreciate it, but it's not right for me," Noir said, reaching his arm over the table in an attempt to touch her hand. She withdrew. *"Baby, you know I'm a contractor—"*

"You've embarrassed me!" she cried, throwing her fork and spoon onto the plate. Everyone must have heard surely, they did—but no one dared to look their way. Yet Noir felt their silent gazes, like a sniper's scope locked on his back. You can't help but shrink under the pressure. *"You've made me look stupid in front of a superior! When will you stop embarrassing me?"*

"I don't!" Noir said. *"I swear I—"*

"Oh, yeah? Then why were you at Sarah's house?" Maddison's words cut through the air like thrown knives.

He tried to defend himself. *"Her boyfriend had passed away—"*

"You were her ex!"

"I know, but I'm still her best friend. She was a wreck, breaking down. I had to console her."

"For a month?"

Noir faltered, unable to find the words.

"And I have to find this out from some random woman?" Maddison snapped. *"How humiliating! What's next? You're going to strip me down and parade me for a walk of shame?"*

"Maddison! That's not fair! You're the one who broke your vow and slept with—"

"Oh, it's not fair?" Maddison shot back, slamming her fists onto the table. *"Where's my house, Noir? Where's my lifetime security? Didn't you promise to treat me like a princess? Why do I have to grind my brain to mush every single day, working like a slave from the old Earth? You said all those things, filled my ears with lies, and now look at me! You tricked me and destroyed my life! Tell me, Noir— where's the fairness in that?"*

Noir's gaze fell to his lap. *"I'm trying. I swear. I'm going to catch a break soon, I know it. You just have to trust me—"*

Maddison nodded, her expression sharp with disdain. She grabbed her purse and slammed it down onto the circular glass panel embedded in the table's surface, transferring digital units to cover their meal. Once finished, she wiped her rosy lips with a napkin. Noir looked on, bewildered, unable to fully process what was unfolding.

Maddison rose abruptly, her chair scraping against the floor. *"You want to keep playing games? Fine, play by yourself. I'm done. We're done. Try to contact me, and I'll call the enforcers. Fuck you!"*

Then she was gone. Noir's head buzzed, his thoughts tangled in static. It felt as though the planet's gravity had multiplied, pressing him down with relentless force. A strange, invisible pain churned within him, like he'd been beaten to a bloody pulp on the inside. His gaze drifted to the chair—empty, as though no one had ever sat there. The sight of its vacancy unsettled him deeply. He wanted it to be full again, wanted it so much that the ache nearly brought him to tears. But no… he wouldn't cry. Deep down, he knew it had been fading for a long time. And now, it was gone—burnt out completely.

A deep sigh escaped from the depths of his soul. This time, he was acutely aware of how it shook him, like a sudden spring gust rattling loose curtains. He turned to scan the room. Every head was turned his way, their gazes heavy and silent.

He rose to his feet and drifted outside like a ghost.

CHAPTER 2

THEY WERE MADE

Noir dreamt of his mother as the darkness of night surrendered to the first light of dawn. Suspended between sleep and wakefulness, he envisioned her bustling in the kitchen, preparing breakfast. He felt the warmth of her kiss on his forehead before she sent him off to school. Her radiant smile, so full of life, lingered in his memory. Those were the days when Father was still alive, and her smile seemed as constant as the rising sun.

Noir's eyes flickered open in the dim glow of the room. To his surprise, his face was damp with tears. *Had I been crying in my sleep?* he wondered.

Noir hadn't seen his mother in twelve years. He thought her memories had gradually faded into oblivion by now. But sitting up in this darkness before dawn, he realized that wasn't the case. Her memories were still vivid, and they rattled him to his core. He sat there, head drooping, staring into the blackness, feeling a void as deep as the space inside his chest, filled with yearning for her. To see the light of her eyes once more, to touch her face for just a second—it gripped him like a gnawing pain. He wasn't expecting to wake up with this strange restlessness clawing at his soul.

Noir lay back down on the bed, staring up at the ceiling, hoping that the restlessness would fade away. His apartment was one of the mass-produced residential units. He could hear the muffled sounds of the city night filtering through the closed window. His bedroom was a cramped space, yet it conveyed the illusion of vastness. They'd used light manipulation techniques to create this absurd effect, designed to ease the feeling of confinement. It seemed as though the ceiling touched the sky when, in reality, it was only thirteen feet above the floor. Even as he stared into that sky-high ceiling, the color of dismal gray, his mind couldn't help but wander back to the extraordinary childhood his mother had given him on another planet. His thoughts began to scatter, slowly drifting back to those days. He could almost feel the plush texture of the couch surrounding him as they snuggled together on rainy afternoons, watching classic films. Her arms were like a warm nest, making him feel safe and cherished. Her soft sweaters carried the scent of delicate perfume and fabric softener. Noir smiled with longing as he remembered the spontaneous road trips they'd take, just for the joy of it. She would start singing along to the radio, and he would join in, their voices blending in cheerful harmony. They'd roll the windows down, letting the rushing air tousle their hair as miles of countryside flew by. Some of his most cherished memories were of the elaborate blanket forts they built in the living room. Propped up by couch cushions and weighed down with books, these shelters became their cozy havens. They would read together for hours, losing themselves in tales of dragons, space pirates, and fantastical realms. Or they would create their own imaginative adventures to pass the time on quiet evenings. A bittersweet ache blossomed within him as he reminisced. Those moments were so simple, but filled with such profound joy and connection. He longed to return, if only for a day, and bask in the pure love and comfort of his mother's embrace. To hear her laughter and soothing voice once more. But he knew those memories would have to sustain him, like glowing embers in the hearth of his heart.

Noir exhaled a weary sigh as he sat up on the edge of his disheveled bed and pressed the button on the bedside panel. Harsh white light flooded the stark room instantly. He rose, the coarse blanket slipping away from his bare form as he padded across the cold metal floor to the expansive window of clear quartz. His eyes narrowed as he surveyed the immense cityscape sprawled out far below. The perpetual atmospheric haze cast an eerie pall, through which the kaleidoscopic lights of the city flickered and danced. The vast network of towering structures and winding streets glowed with an unnatural radioactive luminescence. The skyline stretched as far as the eye could see, a jungle of concrete and steel monoliths interwoven with a maze of cables, pipes, and conduits.

Hovercrafts and drones zipped between the skyscrapers, trailing streaks of light from their thrusters, which flared against the soupy clouds. Down in the maze of streets, teeming masses moved like worker ants, their faces obscured by face masks and AR visors. The air itself seemed to vibrate with the constant hum of the city's activity, punctuated by distant sirens and the unmistakable crack of gunfire. Noir felt small against the sheer scale of the megapolis surrounding him. The entire scene pulsed with the rhythm of human perseverance and progress, yet an undercurrent of corruption and desperation lingered. A reality shaped by overpopulation, unchecked capitalism, and humanity's own self-destructive impulses.

He watched a streak of light arc across the sky, likely an incoming ship. The distant rumble that followed caused the quartz window to vibrate slightly. Noir pressed his palm against the cool glass, somehow feeling even more isolated despite being surrounded by millions of souls in the buzzing metropolis below.

Noir let out another sigh and moved away from the window. He settled into the armchair in the corner and poured some alcohol into a glass. Taking a sip, he absentmindedly reached for the smartphone on the table. Instantly, his mother's 3D image appeared in the air above it. In the projection, she appeared as an eighteen-year-old, her soft skin and red hair blowing in the wind. In her skyblue dress, she looked like an angel who had descended from heaven. She gazed into his eyes and said, *"How are you, my dearest son?"*

Noir knew well that it was merely a 3D holographic image. And he'd seen this clip of hers countless times. Yet the response came out of him automatically, *"I'm well, mother. I'm well."*

In the holographic image, his mother's gaze lingered on him for a few minutes, then she spoke in a soft voice, *"I haven't seen you for so long. You must have grown up, haven't you? You're no longer the little boy I knew. Noir, sometimes, my heart aches for you, and it desperately wants to know where you are, how you're doing."*

Mother lowered her gaze and stared long at her palms, then she spoke in a forlorn voice, *"Wherever you are, Noir, my precious son, my love, I hope you're well and happy."*

Noir's whispering response escaped as though he wanted no one else but his mother to hear, *"Don't you worry, ma, I'm well. I'm happy."*

Tears left her eyes like sudden lightning streaking down across the calm sky. She lifted her hand, rubbed her eyes, and spoke in the most heartbroken, unbearable voice, *"Please don't be mad at this foolish mother of yours, son. I swear I couldn't fathom it; I couldn't understand. If I could, I would have never given birth to you that way. Please believe me—"*

Mother was about to say more as she broke down, but Noir's hand reached out and halted the playback. Despite having watched this clip of his mother a million times, he still could not stand seeing the deep regret and guilt twisting across her face.

When humans could be birthed to a level of superhuman by controlling every single genetic cycle, his mother had given him a natural birth. In a world of superhumans, Noir was born as an ordinary man. His mother could never forgive herself for subjecting him to this unimaginable unfairness. He was always surrounded by people who had been born through careful genetic engineering. Everyone around him was always superior in some way, and compared to them, he was just a regular human being. His mother had unconventional ideas about love and goodness residing within the natural human heart, and she raised him with those values. To her, a good man was the greatest, happiest being in the universe. That's why she underwent the physical changes and endured the incredible pain to give birth naturally, and she tried to raise him to be a good man.

While growing up, Noir discovered that people like him had become obsolete in this stage of human civilization's evolution. He faced obstacles at every turn as he grew. He was denied entry to the prestigious schools, kept away from significant opportunities. Every single day, he had to prove to the authorities that he wasn't a disabled man. When he was just fifteen, he escaped his home planet of Meridian – a planet settled by the human diaspora – to flee this discrimination. He took on numerous jobs, acquiring various skills and studying under many experts since then. He had become a licensed galactic contractor, a person who holds multiple licenses, enabling them to perform a variety of tasks that others cannot. They can adapt to different situations and, most importantly, navigate complex jobs. They were like a one-man enterprise, individuals skilled in many areas, from spaceship piloting to combat, and the best ones were highly valued by the galactic system. Noir was certain his mother would be proud if she saw the person he had become today. She would realize that it didn't matter that she hadn't made her son a superhuman through genetic modification. Everything he had achieved, he fought for and earned through persistence. It's true that he had to endure hardship, but it was never impossible.

He sat there, staring at the empty space above the table where his mother's face once appeared. Then, he pushed all those thoughts aside and stood up. The day had only just begun, and he couldn't afford to waste time.

He was supposed to meet with his client today. He needed to complete his preparations for the upcoming job as well. There were too many things that needed to be put in order. He placed the empty glass on the table and stood up. Just then, a holographic image of an envelope appeared in the air above the table. The message was from Remy Lefevre, the director of the intergalactic voyage department. Noir opened the message; it was marked urgent at the top. He read it and then sighed. This message was more like a government order than a request. They wanted him to handle something for them. It wouldn't matter if he had other jobs to attend to. A summons from the government had to be treated as top priority; ignoring it would be akin to selfsabotage. Noir feared he would have to let down his client.

He prepared himself and met with Remy Lefevre within the hour. The man occupied the corner office. He was a middle-aged, cheerful-looking man with a head full of white hair, seated behind an enormous desk made of genuine teak wood. He raised his hand in greeting and exclaimed as Noir stepped through the doors, *"Ah, Noir! My favorite man in the universe! At last, we meet!"*

Noir couldn't help but laugh as he sat across from him. *"Remy, you talk like meeting me is a matter of luck and a cause for celebration!"*

"Of course, it's a matter of luck! And why wouldn't I celebrate finding a man of your caliber living on this godforsaken planet?"

Noir glanced out the window at the forest of immense skyscrapers. *"No, you would. This world is swarming with life. It's too dense. It's almost become inhospitable. You know what I fear?"*

"What?"

"That all of this is going to collapse someday, and we'll all die like bacteria. Just like what happened to the Nexus Moon colony."

Remy let out a roaring laugh. *"Man, you've got nothing to worry about then! We've made sure you won't have to die like bacteria. We've prepared an Etherean ship to get your ass out of here."*

Noir stared at him. *"You know I don't have the license to pilot an Etherean ship, right?"*

Remy smiled and nodded. *"We'll arrange that license for you as well."*

Noir frowned at the director of the intergalactic voyage department. *"You're just going to hand me an Etherean-class spaceship license, just like that?"*

"Of course. And look," Remy leaned toward Noir over the table, *"this is extremely important right now. Besides, we've analyzed your profile thoroughly, and the entire committee agrees you're perfectly capable*

of handling the responsibility of an Etherean-class spaceship. Sure, you lack the genetic enhancements, but who cares? Look how far you've come. The committee thinks you're a true genius for that, you know. It's about time you got what you deserve."

"Is that so?" Noir fixed him with an intense stare, the kind that seemed to dissect a person's soul. Suspicion bristled in his mind—especially since these pompous government types barely saw people like Noir as human. Remy's words rang false, a poorly constructed illusion. But why? What could he possibly be hiding?

Remy avoided Noir's piercing gaze and said, "Yes, of course! We think it's a fantastic opportunity for you. The next committee might see things differently, and you may not get this chance again. After all, an Etherean-class spaceship could elevate your status across all diaspora planets."

Noir forced a tight smile. "You know, it's funny. My mother never bothered adding any extra cleverness to me through genetic coding before I was born. And maybe I'm not as sharp as everyone else, but even I can tell there's something off about this."

Remy shifted uneasily in his seat. "Like what?"

"I'm trying to figure this out with my limited brain power. You know what? I think it'll all make sense once I know the details of this voyage. First of all, I'm curious— where exactly do you want me to pilot the spaceship?"

Remy hesitated briefly before responding, "To the Veil, in the Solstice region. It's about one hundred and sixty lightyears from Lightlore. I saw your request for a spaceship and noticed you've got a new job in the OB region. Stopping at the Veil on your way to Eorr might be the long way around, but it shouldn't be an issue."

He continued speaking, but Noir flinched. "What did you say? To Solstice?"

Remy's voice grew faint. *"Yes."*

"That means I'll have to go through the Xenosys region?"

"Yes, there's no other way. With two massive black holes on either side, the only viable route is through the Xenosys region. I understand that it's risky to get so close to two massive black holes—"

Noir interrupted sharply, *"You're talking nonsense. For an Etherean spaceship, black holes are nothing during travel. The real danger lies elsewhere."*

Remy's face twisted in surprise. *"Where's the problem?"*

"You know exactly where. Xenosys region has rebelled against Lightlore and the galactic council, declaring themselves independent. That entire region has become a den of criminals, swarming with notorious space bandits. Nearly half the ships that've gone through that region in the last ten years have been robbed. No crew has come back alive."

"You're exaggerating, Noir."

"I'm not exaggerating, not even a little. You people in the government are hiding the real numbers—otherwise, it would be much worse." Noir suddenly felt hot anger bubbling up inside him. He forced himself to keep his tone calm. *"The Xenosys region is hostile for reasons beyond just the space bandits or the black holes. There's some kind of cosmic creature living there—"*

Remy looked confused. *"So what? Species other than humans exist in the cosmos. That's old news."*

"Yes, it's old news," Noir agreed with a nod. *"But if that life form has hostile tendencies—if it's dangerous, if it sees humans and the other species in the Galactic Council as enemies, and if humans don't know anything about it— then we shouldn't go near it. There are clear galactic laws about this. Sending me there would be a violation of those laws."*

Remy's expression darkened, his tone turning cold. *"If you don't want to go, then don't. No one's forcing you to take this mission."*

Hmm, and if I say no, you're going to screw me over like a rogue reactor meltdown, Noir thought, then asked, "What kind of cargo are we talking about here?"

Remy started to respond, but Noir cut him off sharply. "Let me guess—it's going to be toxic, unstable, and outright lethal. The kind of thing you wouldn't lose a wink over if it ended up vaporized mid-transport. Hell, maybe that's the whole point."

Remy's face hardened into something as cold and lifeless as an asteroid. "I think you ought to watch your mouth, Noir. Even my patience has its limits. This cargo is mission-critical."

"And what exactly is it?" Noir pressed.

"We can't disclose that unless you agree to take the mission."

"And I can't agree to anything until I know what I'm hauling."

Remy's glare could've punched through a bulkhead. After a tense moment, he exhaled and muttered, "Alright, fine. Your cargo is... a live human."

"A human?"

"Yes. His name is Humar Danjon. He is—"

"You don't have to tell me who that is. I know."

"I see." Remy nodded.

Noir said sharply, *"So, do you finally see that I was right? My cargo really is toxic, hazardous, and deadly?"*

Remy only stared at me with cold, emotionless eyes.

Noir thought bitterly, These government types. God! They're such insufferable jerks!

Humar Danjon is the most notorious bandit in recent history. He and his crew were the scourge of Xenosys, striking fear into the hearts of its inhabitants. The galactic enforcers had been chasing him for what felt like an eternity, and they only managed to capture him a few days ago. Now, it seems the government plans to send him to the galactic court for trial. They could have just executed him here on this planet, but no—apparently, they'd rather keep this scumbag alive to parade him in front of everyone. Don't they realize that every second he breathes is another chance for chaos to unfold?

Remy asked softly, *"Noir, do you truly not want to take this mission?"*

"Do you think I should feel thrilled about escorting someone like Humar Danjon?"

"But he'll be immobilized, locked away in a titanium vault."

Noir smirked. *"Honestly? If you'd told me I'd get a chance to speak with him during the voyage, I might've been interested."*

"We can't allow that," Remy said, shaking his head firmly. *"No chance."*

"What about my crew?" Noir asked, his tone sharp.

Remy fell silent.

"Let me guess—my crew will be as disposable as I am, right?" Noir shot back.

"Actually, we can't assign you any crew at this time. You'll make the voyage alone."

Noir blinked, stunned. *"What? Alone?"*

"Yes."

"You expect me to complete a mission where I can't even use warp drives because of the black holes—by myself? Alone?" Noir gaped at him, incredulous. *"Have you completely lost it?"*

"It's fine," Remy replied, unfazed. *"These Etherean ships are cutting-edge. Besides, we'll assign you an Artificial Intelligence unit as*

your copilot. You won't even need to lift a finger. The AI will handle everything."

Noir stared at him, silent but fuming.

"Noir, you truly are the best person for this job. The committee has full confidence in you. I can't show you their report, but if I could, you'd see just how highly they regard your abilities."

Noir rose from the plush chair with a deliberate calm. *"Thank you for your confidence, Remy. But I'm afraid I can't take your job. I've got a contract I need to handle. Have a good day."*

He turned on his heel and strode toward the door. Just as his hand pushed it open, Remy's voice stopped him.

"Noir," Remy said with a curious smile that hinted at knowledge he wasn't yet sharing. *"I think you'll agree to this mission in the end."*

Noir glanced back, raising an eyebrow. *"And why is that?"*

Remy leaned back in his chair, his smile deepening. *"Because you've got a message."*

Noir frowned slightly. *"A message?"*

"That's correct," Remy confirmed.

"From whom?" Noir's voice was measured but carried a flicker of curiosity.

"Your mother."

Noir felt his pulse quicken, his composure wavering for the first time. *"My mother?"* he echoed, disbelief creeping into his tone.

"Yes," Remy said with certainty.

Noir's voice tightened, barely concealing his unease. *"What did she say?"*

"It's for you," Remy replied, his expression betraying a trace of satisfaction. *"The intergalactic communication department just delivered it."* He opened a drawer of his genuine wooden desk and retrieved a

small circular disk. With a quick flick of his wrist, he tossed it across the room like a frisbee.

Noir caught the disk effortlessly, his eyes narrowing at the unexpected turn of events. His gaze snapped back to Remy, whose smirk was now unmistakable. *"It came from Meridian,"* Remy added, his tone casual but his words weighted. *"Which, coincidentally, is very close to the mission's destination—Veil."*

Remy rose from his chair and walked to the transparent wall, his gaze drifting over the sprawling megacity below. For a moment, he seemed lost in thought, the hum of the city reflecting faintly against the glass. Then, he turned sharply, locking eyes with Noir. His voice carried an unfamiliar edge as he said, *"Noir, I don't think you understand just how fortunate you are. You were born inside a real mother's womb. Do you want to know how I came into existence? I wasn't born. I was engineered—in a genetics lab. The same way machines are built."*

Noir couldn't tear his gaze away from Remy's face. The cold, calculating man who had always seemed unshakable now carried an unexpected weight of sadness.

CHAPTER 3

MESSAGE FROM MERIDIAN

Noir sat in the armchair, back in his dimly lit apartment. He touched the smartphone, and the playback began. Above the table, a holographic projection of his mother flickered to life, vivid and startlingly real. For a fleeting moment, Noir felt an ache in his chest, a desperate longing to reach out, almost believing he could touch her.

The hologram showed his mother gazing at the rolling waves of a distant ocean. She turned slowly, her piercing eyes meeting the camera as she spoke. *"Noir, my son. I don't know if you can see me. I don't even know where in the vastness of the universe you might be right now. Even so, I like to imagine you're sitting before me—still and quiet, like the good boy you've always been—listening to every word I say."*

She paused, a gentle laugh escaping her lips, as if she could truly see him sitting there. Her youthful appearance was striking; she looked like a teenager, her features seemingly untouched by time. She had always carried herself with an energy that belied her years.

She let out a long sigh, her voice soft, and for a moment, the sound of crashing waves filled the silence.

Then her expression changed. Her fiery red hair whipped in the wind as she pushed it back, her tone shifting to something somber. *"You know, son, I've been feeling this strange, gnawing restlessness lately. It's like I can't shake the questions running through my mind—the ones about why we're here, what it all means. Was I born just to exist for a fleeting moment, like a spark that fades into nothingness? Is this all there is, or is there something deeper, some purpose waiting to be uncovered?"*

Her voice lowered as she continued. *"The purpose of the animal kingdom across the cosmos seems simple enough—to reproduce, to multiply. But that's not true for us, for humankind, is it? Humans don't even need to be born anymore. They design infants in genome factories, tailored to precise specifications. So, if survival and reproduction aren't our sole reasons for existence, what is? Why do we keep going, son? What's the reason behind it all?"*

Mother paused, her eyes fixed on the camera, as if she were peering directly into Noir's soul. He couldn't look away. With the rhythmic crash of ocean waves behind her, her fiery hair dancing in the wind, and her piercing blue eyes locked on him, Noir found himself utterly captivated. That's why her sudden burst of laughter caught him off guard.

"You know what's funny?" she said, her voice light with amusement. *"Everyone around me is so worried about me! They see these odd thoughts and questions filling my mind, and now they're convinced I need some sort of treatment!"* She laughed again, the sound almost contagious. *"One day, they nearly dragged me to an artificial intelligence doctor. It ran a bunch of tests, did whatever it does."*

She paused, a mischievous smile playing on her lips before she continued, *"And you know what the AI doc said to me?"* She giggled, the laughter bubbling up again. *"It said I need an AI chip implanted in my brain. To control my thoughts. Can you believe that? Basically, it wanted to turn me into a robot!"*

Mother's laughter was unstoppable, spilling out in an unrestrained, childlike way that lit up the moment. It was so infectious that Noir found himself laughing along with her, the sound filling the room as if it bridged the distance between them.

When her laughter finally subsided, she wiped the tears from her eyes and said, *"Of course, I told that robot doctor to shut itself down. No AI chip got implanted in this brain of mine. What you see here is one hundred percent pure gray matter."* She tapped her temple lightly, a playful smirk on her face. *"And because of that, I still have all these strange, restless thoughts."*

She paused, her expression softening with a tinge of worry. *"Noir, you're not getting bored listening to all this, are you?"*

Noir shook his head, his voice barely a whisper. *"No, Ma. I could never."*

She smiled, but her voice carried a hint of urgency. *"It's okay if you are. It doesn't matter. I just want to talk to you. I don't know why, but I feel like you'd understand me if you were here. You'd know what I mean."* Her smile faded as her tone grew heavy. *"No one here understands me. They all think I'm crazy."*

Her gaze shifted, as if looking for answers in the distance. *"I used to believe the purpose of life was to seek knowledge. But have you seen who's made the biggest discoveries and inventions over the past hundred years? Robots, computers, artificial intelligence. Even the breakthroughs credited to humans were made possible by machines—*

hypermind calculators and other advanced systems." She looked back at the camera, her voice trembling slightly. "*So what's left for us, Noir? What's left for just humans? Why should we keep going? What's the purpose of our lives?*"

Mother shook her head, a faint smile tugging at her lips. "*I don't even know why I'm rambling like this. I'm not sure if it's really you I'm speaking to. Then why? Because I need to share my thoughts with someone, and in all the universe, it feels like you're the only one who would understand me. I imagine you're sitting right here, close to me.*"

She paused, her expression softening as she continued. "*These days, my thoughts have shifted. I no longer believe life has no meaning. I used to think that giving you a natural birth was the greatest mistake of my life—that I should've designed you in a lab like everyone else does. I no longer believe that. I don't regret not making you a superhuman. I raised you with care and poured all my love into your heart.*"

Her smile grew tender as her voice steadied. "*Who said everyone has to be the best? Everyone has their own purpose. No one is unnecessary in this universe. Together, we all contribute to its existence.*" She chuckled softly. "*I suppose I've said some pretty lofty things, haven't I? But I think I've earned the right to pester you like this. You're my son. I carried you in my womb, nourished you through my placenta, and gave you life.*"

Her gaze grew distant, thoughtful. "*You know, Noir, so many questions about life flood my mind, but there's no one to answer them. You have to find those answers yourself. But there was someone who helped me a great deal—her name was Elise Martin. She lived in the Hazemaze colony. She died three hundred years ago. If she were still alive, I would've done whatever it took to meet her.*"

"*She wrote books, research papers, and even recorded video clips. I studied all of them carefully, trying to grasp her ideas. She was so incredibly intelligent, almost impossibly brilliant. It felt as though each neuron in her brain had been arranged by some divine hand. After immersing myself in her work, I finally found answers to many of the questions that have haunted me.*

"And then, I discovered something new a few days ago. They mapped her entire brain before she died—three hundred years ago! Did you know they do this with legendary philosophers, scientists, and artists? They preserve their minds by creating these detailed maps. Which means that even though Elise Martin is no longer alive, her brain essentially is! If you connect it to a massive hypermind calculator, you can actually talk to her. Isn't that incredible?

"But here's the sad part. There aren't many hypermind calculators capable of running human brain maps. And the few that exist are completely out of reach for people like us. You'd need to be a high-status citizen to access one." Mother laughed, the sound light but tinged with resignation. *"Listen to me, going on and on like this. I guess I think you'll be curious about these strange things too, just like I am. But forget everything I said, my son. Treat it as the ramblings of a madwoman.*

"Please, if you ever find the time, come visit me. I want to show everyone my only son—the son I carried in my body, the son I love more than anything in the universe."

Mother fell silent, gazing at Noir with a warm smile. Slowly, her expression began to falter. Her lips trembled, and tears gathered at the corners of her eyes, though she tried to blink them away. Then, the message ended.

As the holographic image faded, Noir felt that familiar emptiness spreading across his chest again. He reached for his smartphone, activating it with a single touch. This time, the hologram displayed Remy's face, sharp and inquisitive.

Remy studied him for a moment, a question in his eyes. *"What's up, Noir? Have you made your decision?"*

"Yes. I'll go."

"Excellent," Remy said with a satisfied nod. *"Then there's no point in delaying any further. You'll leave tomorrow morning. We've already lost enough time, as I'm sure you understand. One of our scout ships from Astro Station Four will take you to the Wayfarer."*

"The Wayfarer?" Noir asked.

Remy's lips curled into a faint smile. *"Yes, our latest model Etherean-class spaceship. It's been parked in stable orbit."*

"In orbit?" Noir echoed, his brow furrowing slightly.

"That's right," Remy replied. *"Etherean-class ships are never brought down to a planet's surface."*

"Okay." Noir hesitated for a moment. *"Remy?"*

"Yes?"

"If I ask you a question, will you answer truthfully?"

Remy smiled again, this time with a touch of caution. *"I can't promise you an answer without hearing the question first. Sometimes, masking the truth is necessary for survival."*

Noir's gaze hardened. *"The things I said to you earlier about the Xenosys region… they're all true, aren't they?"*

Remy paused, his face unreadable. Finally, he said, *"Does it really matter?"*

"No," Noir said quietly. *"Not anymore."*

"Then let's not discuss it any further," Remy concluded, his tone firm.

* * *

"Yeah, I just signed the papers. It's over," Noir said, seated on the park bench. Sarah's arms were wrapped around him, her head resting gently on his shoulder. *"These past couple of years were a lie."*

"I'm sorry, sweetheart," she said softly. Her hair carried the faint scent of daisies, and her voice, like the song of a bird, brought a soothing balm to his scorched heart. *"Something like this should never have happened to you. You're the sweetest, most caring person I know. I'm so sorry."*

"Thank you." Noir kissed her hair lightly. *"Well, whatever. I have to leave anyway. Ma's becoming unstable—I need to go see her. I can't believe I ignored her all these years. I'm such a bad son. Maybe this is karma getting back at me—"*

Sarah lifted her head from his shoulder, meeting his eyes with a steady gaze. *"Sweetheart, you don't mean that."*

Noir chuckled, his voice tinged with a faint sadness. *"I don't. I'm just talking."*

Sarah rested her head back on his shoulder. *"Don't ever talk like that."*

"I won't. I promise."

"When will you be leaving?" she asked after a pause.

"I don't know. Probably in a week."

"Maybe it's for the best," she said softly. *"You'll be able to throw yourself into work and leave all this behind."*

"I sincerely hope so. Speaking of which, I still haven't updated my client about my situation. I better go do that now."

They separated, both standing from the bench.

"Hey," Noir said, his voice gentler now, *"thank you for lending me a shoulder to cry on. I feel a lot better."*

"Anything for you," she said, leaning in and kissing him deeply. The kiss lingered, their connection palpable in the stillness of the moment. Then, she slowly pulled away. *"Now, go do your job. And keep all those stupid thoughts out of your head, you hear me?"*

Noir nodded, a faint smile tugging at the corners of his lips. *"See you around, Sarah."*

Without another word, he turned and walked away, the weight of their parting settling in as he made his way back to his apartment.

* * *

"So, as you can see, I'll need some time before I can attend to your request," Noir explained, seated in his apartment on the armchair, speaking to his client, Lynthex Gumshoe.

The holographic image of Lynthex showed him visibly distressed. He was outside, sitting at a table in a bustling square as Eorrian people moved around him in a constant stream. *"The issue is, Noir, I'm not entirely sure about the nature of the job myself. It could be urgent, or it could turn out to be trivial. So, I don't want to cancel your contract. I'll keep it open for now."*

"I'm sorry, I'm not sure I follow," Noir said, his brow furrowing. *"You don't know the nature of the job?"*

"Well, I do, sort of. I need you to investigate something for me, but I'm not sure what I'm looking for exactly. Now, look, we can't discuss this in detail over the communication link. I'll tell you everything I know once we meet in person. But I suppose I'm a bit concerned in case the situation turns out to be serious."

"I truly apologize, Mr. Gumshoe," Noir said, his voice tinged with regret. *"I'd like nothing more than to attend to your request immediately, but I lack the authority to decline a direct assignment—"*

Mr. Gumshoe raised his hand, cutting him off. *"Yeah, yeah, I get it. I may be a politician, but let me tell you, I'm not a fan of strongarming people. At any rate, try to wrap it up quickly, will ya?"*

"I'll do my best, sir," Noir said, bowing his head slightly.

"How long do you need, anyway?" Lynthex asked, his tone edged with impatience.

"No longer than a month," Noir replied. Seeing the shock on Lynthex's face, he quickly added, *"Unfortunately, the presence of the two massive black holes complicates the mission and prevents us from engaging the warp drives. If everything proceeds according to schedule, the mission will be complete, and I'll be back on the planet of Eorr within a month."*

Lynthex sighed, his frustration evident. *"I suppose it can't be helped, then. Well, I'll be anxiously waiting for you. There are precious few contractors I trust with this kind of job, and your name is at the top of the list, Noir. I need you handling this—even if I have to wait a month, I'll begrudgingly do so. The nature of the issue is that delicate."*

"I understand, sir." Noir straightened in his seat, meeting his client's gaze with steady determination. *"I will do everything in my power to reach Eorr in thirty days. You have my word."*

"Alright, I guess I'll see you then." Lynthex tipped his hat. *"Take care."*

The holographic image flickered and vanished as the link was terminated. Noir let out a long breath before rising from his seat. Without hesitation, he left his apartment, heading to meet his new spaceship.

* * *

Noir stood in awe at the sight of the spaceship *Wayfarer*. It was colossal, rivaling the size of a small satellite. Its exterior was forged from an alloy of titanium and chromium, encased in a layer of cutting-edge material that completely resisted heat conduction. The main engine ran on matter-antimatter fuel, with massive plasma engines reserved for emergencies. It also boasted the latest in intergalactic communication technology, capable of transmitting across unfathomable distances.

But what truly humbled Noir was the *Wayfarer's* sublime hypermind calculator—a machine so advanced it could control every aspect of the ship with a precision no human could rival. Standing before it, Noir couldn't help but feel insignificant. The vast potential of the human mind seemed almost trivial compared to the towering intellect of the hypermind.

The defining feature of an Etherean-class spaceship like the *Wayfarer* was its versatility. It combined the best attributes of other classes: the immense cargo capacity of a Lattice-class ship, the unparalleled processing power of a Matrix-class vessel, and an arsenal rivaling a Terminatorclass warship, including nuclear blasters, laser arrays, and more. Thankfully, Noir wasn't expected to operate all of this on his own. The hypermind would handle the heavy lifting— managing navigation, weapons, and logistics—while Noir needed only to issue commands.

Barely given a moment to catch his breath, Noir was thrust into the demanding role of commanding the *Wayfarer*. To cope with the overwhelming responsibilities, he resorted to taking the brain-enhancing drug *"Stimuvate,"* pushing himself to work for six straight days without a single moment of sleep.

When the crew threw a party to celebrate his certification as a new Etherean pilot, Noir was barely present in the moment. As they handed him his license, he drifted into a trance-like state, a side effect of accumulated fatigue and the lingering influence of Stimuvate. The events of the party blurred together in his mind, leaving him unsure of what he did or even how he made it back to his quarters.

Not even a drug as potent as Stimuvate could keep him going indefinitely. The moment his body hit the bed, exhaustion consumed him, and he sank into a deep, dreamless sleep.

After being unconscious for forty-eight hours, Noir's senses were assaulted as he slowly regained consciousness. His eyelids felt heavy, crusted from lingering sleep. When he managed to peel them open, the dim light filtering through the curtains stabbed at his sensitive eyes. He blinked rapidly, trying to moisten them, but the dryness persisted, making the effort almost painful.

His mouth was unbearably dry, his tongue rough like sandpaper scraping against the roof of his mouth. He dragged it across his cracked, peeling lips, tasting the stale bitterness of dehydration and prolonged sleep. As he inhaled deeply through his nose, a musty, sour odor hit him—a mix of his own sweat and the stagnant air of the cold room. His nostrils flared as he struggled to find a trace of freshness.

His head pounded relentlessly, each throb in sync with the rapid beat of his heart. Dull aches radiated from his temples, spreading with every sluggish turn of his heavy head on the flat pillow. His muscles were lifeless, weighed down as if he'd been strapped with lead while he slept. When he tried to move, his joints creaked and popped in protest, sending sharp twinges of pain through his sluggish body.

The cold that had seeped into the room while he was unconscious hit Noir's exposed skin in sharp, prickly waves. Goosebumps rippled across his body as it struggled to generate warmth after two days of total inertia.

But overriding the chill was the ravenous pang of hunger clawing at his stomach—a hollow, gnawing ache amplified by the sour churn of acids. His belly gurgled loudly, a relentless demand for sustenance after such prolonged deprivation.

He punched the bedside panel, staring at it in disbelief. He thought he'd been out for only a few hours, but no—the display informed him he had slept for forty-eight hours straight. His smartphone, resting on the table nearby, was projecting a steady stream of urgent notifications.

Noir groaned as he forced himself upright, stumbling toward the table. His body felt alien, like he had possessed a corpse and was struggling to make it move.

He collapsed into his armchair and touched his smartphone. Instantly, a hologram of Remy's frightened face flickered into the air.

"Noir! Are you alright, man? What happened to you?" Remy's voice was tinged with anxiety.

"Sleeping," Noir slurred, his words sluggish and disjointed. *"Took Stimuvate. Stayed awake for days. Etherean training. Body just… stopped working."*

Remy nodded, his expression softening with understanding. *"Yeah, I figured it might be something like that. But I didn't think you'd be out for so long."*

"Me neither," Noir muttered, pulling himself out of the armchair. *"Why did you call?"* He shuffled toward his provision unit and yanked it open.

"We don't have any more time. You need to start your voyage right now."

"What do you mean 'right now'? When is this 'right now'?" Noir asked, his tone sharpening as he grabbed a bottle of green, nutrient-packed liquid. Popping the cork, he gulped it down greedily, the cool liquid soothing the raw dryness in his throat.

"Within the next twenty-four hours. A massive magnetic storm is heading this way. If we don't get you out before it arrives, it'll be too late."

Noir put down the bottle. The liquid was delicious, and he could feel a refreshing surge of energy spreading through his body. *"I understand, but I have some preparations to take care of myself."*

"No," Remy said firmly. *"There's no need for you to handle preparations on your own. We've already taken care of everything on your behalf."*

"But I had personal matters—"

Remy's tone grew sharp with impatience. *"The moment you signed up for this mission, you relinquished anything 'personal.' We've got your entire profile in our database. We know everything about you, Noir. The Wayfarer has been configured to your exact preferences. You'll find all your favorite books, foods, clothes, music— everything you could possibly need. There's nothing left for you to handle."*

"But—"

"No buts," Remy interrupted. *"Besides, you'll be able to maintain contact with everyone in the network right up until the Wayfarer hits extreme velocity."*

Noir hesitated, his lips tightening. Finally, he said, *"Actually, there's something else I wanted to bring with me on the voyage."*

Remy raised an eyebrow. *"What is it?"*

"The brain mapping of Elise Martin."

Remy's jaw dropped in astonishment, and he let out a low whistle. *"You're serious?"*

Noir shifted uneasily. *"Can I not have it?"*

Remy exhaled, rubbing the back of his neck. *"It's going to be difficult, but I'll see what I can do."*

"'Seeing what you can do' isn't good enough," Noir said, his voice steady but firm. *"I must have it. You know I'm risking my life on this mission, Remy. And let's not forget—I'll be completely alone on that ship. No crew, no company. Having someone—or something—to talk to would make all the difference."*

Remy burst out laughing. *"You're not going to be away for that long."*

"It doesn't matter. It's all the same to me," Noir said, his tone grim. *"There's Humar Danjon, and there's the Xenosys region. Anything could happen on this voyage. It's the most dangerous mission I've ever attempted."*

"Sure, I get it," Remy replied, his smile fading.

Noir leaned forward, his voice sharp and deliberate. *"Listen, Remy. If I don't get Elise Martin's brain mapping, I'm not going on this voyage."*

Remy groaned in frustration. *"Oh, come on, man! Now you're just blackmailing me like one of those damned space bandits!"*

"It's not blackmail. It's the truth," Noir shot back.

Remy exhaled, rubbing his temples. *"Alright, alright, fine. I'll get it for you."*

"There's one more thing I need."

Remy rolled his eyes. *"Please, no more impossible demands."*

"It's not impossible," Noir said calmly. *"I want a good luck bonsai tree in a quartz sphere. I want to take it as a gift for my mom, along*

with Elise Martin's brain mapping. It's a special tree that only grows on the planet Lightlore. A small tree with countless tiny blue petals. People say it only blooms with a bright orange flower when something miraculous happens in the owner's life. It's one of the most beautiful things in the universe."

Remy raised an eyebrow but nodded. *"Well, that's quite the luxury item, but it's doable. You're a high-status citizen now, after all."*

"That's great!" Noir said, a flicker of relief in his voice. *"There's no regulation against carrying trees or living plants during an intergalactic voyage like this, is there?"*

Remy laughed. *"You're carrying Humar Danjon in your spaceship as cargo. If you're allowed to bring something like that, you're definitely allowed a tree. Don't worry about it."*

"Alright, I'll leave it to you," Noir said with a nod.

"Good," Remy replied. *"Head to Astro Station Four. We'll begin the preparations for your departure now. You've got no more than one hour."*

"One hour?" Noir echoed, his voice rising. *"I'm supposed to leave an entire planet in just one hour?"*

Remy sighed heavily. *"If someone gave me the chance to escape this dystopian cesspool, I'd leave in under a minute."*

Noir stared at the man, his expression unreadable. The chaotic lights from outside streamed through Remy's window, casting shifting patterns across his face and giving him an otherworldly, almost alien appearance.

For a fleeting moment, Noir wondered if there was some truth to his words.

Chapter 4

Personality is Enigma

The vault's inner layer was constructed from an exceptionally strong titanium alloy. Between this inner layer and the outer black steel shell, multiple layers of advanced materials, mechanisms, and technologies were meticulously designed to work in unison. These layers ensured that the occupant inside remained as immobile and solid as a frozen block of ice.

The enforcers maneuvered the large, specially engineered vault into the spacecraft using a floating transport machine. They carefully secured the rectangular structure into the designated slot in the wall. Once the task was completed, the head enforcer officer stepped forward and announced, "This is the super-reinforced vault holding the criminal known as Humar Danjon. I now officially transfer it to Noir Legend, captain and pilot of the Etherean-class spaceship *Wayfarer*."

Noir, floating in the zero-gravity environment of the spacecraft, drifted toward the vault. He rested a hand on its cold, metallic surface and said, *"I've heard so many strange stories about this human that I want to be absolutely certain he doesn't wake up during our flight."*

The enforcer officer laughed. *"You can relax about that. He'll remain frozen at an extremely cold liquid helium temperature. No human can possibly wake up under those conditions—it's completely impossible."*

"Maybe it's impossible for regular humans like you and me," Noir replied, his voice edged with doubt. *"But when it comes to Humar Danjon? I'm not so sure."*

The officer's expression remained calm as he said, *"You can rest assured. The laws of physics apply to Humar Danjon just as they do to you and me. At liquid helium temperatures, the biological processes inside a human body cease entirely. He is, quite literally, an inanimate object now."*

Noir paused, considering this explanation. *"What if someone tries to send him a signal from the outside? Could that wake him up?"*

The officer shook his head confidently. *"No. No one can send any signal or data into this cube. It's completely shielded against external signals or interference. You can consider it secure."*

Satisfied for the moment, Noir nodded as the enforcer officer turned to the onboard hypermind. After completing the official procedures, the officer approached Noir and handed him a small cube device. *"Noir, you now have the clearance to begin your voyage."*

Noir accepted the device, glancing at the rows of regular cylinders lining the walls—countless of them, arranged with cold precision. Many other people were here in cryosleep alongside Humar Danjon. Some were civilians, while others were not. Noir knew he could access all their identities in the hypermind if he wanted, but why bother?

There were also vaults in the ship carrying things far stranger than humans, but their contents weren't his concern. As the captain of the *Wayfarer,* his job was simple: transport all of this cargo safely to its destination.

Of course, Humar Danjon was an exception. His presence was unique and required constant vigilance. Even if the man was reduced to an inanimate object, a spaceship captain had to remain acutely aware of having someone like him onboard.

The enforcer and the technicians who had accompanied him began packing up their equipment. Organizing everything in a zero-gravity environment was no small feat, but Noir couldn't help being fascinated by their skillful, meticulous work. One by one, they finished their tasks and prepared to say their goodbyes.

Each of them approached Noir, shaking his hand or offering a brief hug, their words of encouragement varying but sincere. The enforcer officer was the last to step forward. Gripping Noir's hand firmly, he gave it a small squeeze and said, *"I hope you have a safe voyage, Noir."*

Noir offered a meaningful smile. *"I'll do my best to make that happen. Thank you."*

The enforcer officer nodded and left with the rest of the team. Once everyone had boarded the scout ship, Noir sealed the circular airtight door behind them. Through the transparent window, he watched as the scout ship silently drifted away, its sleek form glowing against the backdrop of the dazzling planet Lightlore, sparkling like a cluster of fireflies in the dark.

Now, Noir was alone.

A peculiar melancholy settled in the depths of his soul, creeping in like an insidious whisper. He contemplated the vast distances that lay before him, the isolation of his voyage inside the Wayfarer. He would traverse the chasm of space, journeying from one distant star to another, alone in the void.

The great vessel would propel forward into the black infinity, its engines roaring against the silence of the abyss. What perils awaited him in the sprawling darkness? Noir shuddered at the thought. The path ahead was treacherous, fraught with hazardous orbits where massive black holes reigned supreme, their gravitational pull a siren call to all who ventured too close. And then, there were the space bandits, lurking just beyond the Xenosys region, ready to plunder anything—and anyone—who crossed their path, even taking lives without hesitation.

And what of the unknown, the unfathomable entities that dwelled beyond the grasp of human understanding? Would he encounter such beings—aliens from hostile worlds? Even in this age of intelligence supremacy, vast stretches of the universe remained cloaked in ignorance, untouched by human comprehension.

Noir trembled at the thought. Anything could happen on this voyage, and if it did, he and everyone aboard would be lost to the endless void of space. Cast adrift in an eternal, starless sea. The distances they traveled seemed deceptively small, thanks to warp drives that bent space and time, and lore drives that enabled faster-than-light travel through normal space. Yet those same distances were unimaginably vast. If something went wrong, if the spaceship malfunctioned, that *"small"* distance would stretch into an infinite, hopeless expanse. It could leave them stranded among the stars, forever lost. Would he ever reach the Solstice region? Would he ever see his mother's face one last time? Or would that dream of reunion remain forever out of reach?

Noir gritted his teeth and shoved the thoughts away, forcing them out of his mind like invasive weeds. Swimming in the zero-gravity environment, he began making his way to the upper level of the spaceship. He had to reach the control room and prepare for departure immediately. He needed to secure himself in a safe position before the *Wayfarer's* engines roared to life, tearing the ship free from the planet's gravitational pull and hurling it toward the endless depths of the cosmos.

As Noir settled into the plush, unnervingly comfortable chair before the main control panel, the voice of the hypermind calculator broke the silence. *"On behalf of the Etherean-class spaceship Wayfarer, I humbly invite you to officially assume command of this spaceship, Your Highness Noir."*

A shiver ran up Noir's spine, a creeping unease spreading through his body. There was something profoundly unsettling about a machine mimicking human speech. Something about it felt wrong—uncanny, even unnatural. It scratched at the edges of his psyche in a way that human voices never did. He wished the developers understood the importance of maintaining a strict, unmistakable distinction between the speech of humans and machines. Humans could be seen, understood, and empathized with as they spoke, their words infused with emotion and intent. Machines, however, were something else entirely. Talking to a machine felt like conversing with an entity devoid of a soul, an unknowable presence. Could you ever truly understand what you were speaking with?

Noir had always been deeply unsettled by this question.

He strapped himself into the chair with the security belts and said, *"And what if I told you I reject your invitation?"*

The hypermind replied in an amused tone, *"Your Highness Noir, you have the right to do that, of course. But please note that you've already signed the mission contract with the government of Lightlore. My invitation holds no significance—I'm merely a tool to assist you on this voyage."*

"And who exactly is this 'you'?" Noir asked, his tone laced with curiosity.

"My name is Enigma. You may call me Eni for short. Eni is the link module connecting the Wayfarer's hypermind and its human captain."

Noir leaned forward against the control panel, his fingers moving across the buttons with practiced precision. *"Tell me something, Eni,"* he said, his voice almost playful. *"What if I started cursing you out, using the most vile and revolting words I know? Would you flip out on me? Would you stop functioning?"*

"Not at all, Your Highness Noir," Eni replied, its tone remaining calm and measured. *"I am not a human being. I cannot be offended or slighted by someone's words or actions. I am unable to perceive disrespectful or demeaning gestures. The purpose of my existence is to assist you, and I will fulfill that purpose in the best possible way."*

Noir was checking the status report on the *Wayfarer's* engines and other critical systems. *"Eni, as far as I know, your hypermind is far more advanced than a human brain. It's said that your intelligence is about twelve times greater than that of the average human. Which means you're actually much smarter than I am. So, it's only fair that I start addressing you as Your Highness Eni—"*

Eni laughed. Her laughter was like the sound of crystal wind chimes dancing in a gentle breeze—pure and shimmering. *"I think you've misunderstood, Your Highness Noir,"* she said. *"I am not the hypermind. I'm merely a link module that connects the hypermind* to the human captain. If you imagine the hypermind as a human being, then I am simply its voice. I have no intelligence of my own.

"Besides, Your Highness Noir, formal addressing has no significance. Research has shown that when a human and a machine work together on a task, prioritizing the human makes the entire process more straightforward and efficient."

"Oh, I see," Noir said, exhaling a long sigh. *"Well, it looks like the two of us are stuck with each other for a long time, Eni. We'll have plenty of time to argue about man versus machine. For now, let's fire up the Wayfarer."*

"Understood."

Once the system check was complete, Noir activated the twin engines. Instantly, the two massive thrusters mounted on either side of the *Wayfarer* roared to life, filling the ship with a deep, resonant thrum. The entire vessel vibrated like a living beast, trembling with incomprehensible power. Through the transparent window, Noir watched the ionized gas erupting from the engines in streams of blinding thunderbolts. He had ignited countless spaceship engines in his lifetime, but for the first time, he felt the immense force resonate through every fiber of his being.

The *Wayfarer* rumbled and vibrated as if Noir were seated within the belly of a raging giant, screaming defiance at the heavens. The ship began its final orbit around the planet. Before completing its circle, the twin engines would rip free from the planet's gravitational hold and launch into the vast expanse of space.

Noir sat in his chair, his gaze fixed on the glowing control panel. The zero-gravity environment began to fade, replaced by an intense pull as the ship accelerated. It felt as though some invisible, godlike force was telekinetically pinning him to the plush, ergonomic chair.

Noir had always been able to endure higher gravitational forces than most— a mystery his master had once attributed to his ferrionics.

As the acceleration peaked, the G-forces bore down on him like an unrelenting, colossal weight. It was as if an unseen boulder were pressing against his chest, making every breath an exhausting battle. Noir's body grew impossibly heavy, the crushing forces stacking relentlessly upon him. He gasped for air, his lungs straining against the invisible mass constricting his chest. A bead of warm sweat rolled down his temple, cutting a path through the mounting pressure as he struggled to endure the unyielding forces.

Eni's voice whispered softly near Noir's ear, *"Your Highness Noir, with your consent, I can administer anesthetic drugs to render you unconscious for a period of time."*

Noir gritted his teeth and replied with unwavering determination, "No!"

"But why? Why endure so much pain?" Eni asked, her tone almost imploring.

"I don't know," Noir admitted through clenched teeth.

"Your Highness, soon blood flow to your brain will cease, and you will lose consciousness on your own."

"Even so," Noir said, his voice strained. *"I wish to see."*

A reddish veil began to flicker before his eyes, his vision narrowing and growing hazy around the edges. His face felt unnaturally tight, as if his skin were retracting under the relentless forces acting upon him. Noir's eyelids grew heavier with each excruciating second, the effort to keep them open becoming an unwinnable battle.

Eni whispered again, her voice tinged with a hint of desperation, *"But Your Highness, you must be put under— for the sake of your own safety. This is pure madness—"* *"I know!"* Noir snapped.

"But Your Highness—"

"Eni!" Noir barked, his voice trembling with defiance. *"Do machines ever do this? Can a machine ever be crazy?"*

Noir didn't hear Eni's response.

With one final, shallow inhalation, the world faded to black. Noir slumped back in his seat, unconscious, as the merciless G-forces overwhelmed his body's fragile resistance against the crushing acceleration.

* * *

By the time Noir regained consciousness, the spaceship *Wayfarer* was already cruising toward its fixed destination. Inside the vessel, a comfortable gravitational pull had been established. Noir unbuckled the safety belts and stepped down to the floor. *"Eni?"* he called out.

"Yes, Your Highness Noir?"

"Everything running smoothly?"

"Yes, Your Highness Noir. Are you feeling well?"

"There's a dull pain in my head, but I'm hoping it will go away soon," Noir replied. He turned to gaze out through the transparent window at the rapidly shrinking planet in the distance. It was hard for him to fathom how so many people lived their entire lives confined to tiny apartments on that fragile blue orb, floating aimlessly in the vast emptiness of space.

Noir's eyes drifted toward the peculiar miniature tree nearby. It was unmistakably a bonsai, though unlike any he had encountered before. Delicate tendrils of pale blue foliage trembled faintly, as though sensing an imperceptible breeze despite the stillness of the cabin. The gnarled trunk and branches seemed to twist and curl into mesmerizing, fractallike patterns, defying the natural rules of botany.

As Noir leaned in closer, he realized the bonsai was encased in a perfectly clear sphere of glass or crystal, nestled securely within a transparent case. The tiny azure leaves quivered, almost as if they were apprehensive about embarking on the long and uncertain voyage ahead. Despite its ethereal, alien beauty, the bonsai exuded a quiet mystery that made Noir hold his breath in awe.

Noir gestured toward the tree and asked, *"Is this the famous good luck tree?"*

"Yes, Your Highness Noir," Eni confirmed. *"That is the good luck tree."*

"So, this tree blossoms a flower when someone is blessed with good luck?"

"There's an urban legend to that effect," Eni replied.

"Do you believe it?" Noir asked, his gaze lingering on the tree's trembling leaves.

Eni paused, her voice measured as she replied, *"I think it becomes believable once you redefine what it means to have good luck."*

"How so?" Noir asked.

"For example, you might consider that witnessing a flower blooming on this strange tree is a miracle in itself," Eni replied.

Noir burst out laughing. *"Well said, Eni. Well said. You are certainly very clever."*

"Thank you, Your Highness Noir."

Noir circled the transparent case, his gaze lingering on the bizarrely beautiful miniature tree. *"I'm bringing this good luck tree to my mom as a gift."*

"I know," Eni said.

"What do you think, Eni? Do you think my mother will like it?"

"Of course she will."

"How can you be so sure? You've never even met my mother," Noir countered.

"Because your mother will value the fact that you brought her a gift from across the universe. It wouldn't matter to her what kind of gift it is. Besides, there's a certain charm in the name 'good luck tree.' Humans enjoy waiting for a miracle."

Noir smiled faintly. *"It sounds like you know humans really well."*

"It may come naturally to you humans, but we machines have to learn to understand you," Eni replied.

Noir moved away from the quivering good luck tree and approached the observatory window. Outside, the void of space consumed everything, an infinite expanse of inky blackness. Thousands of stars blinked and flickered like merry little fireflies, scattered across the bottom of a vast, endless inkwell.

As Noir planted his feet firmly on the deck, he felt the faint, barely perceptible vibrations of the spacecraft's powerful engines humming through the soles of his boots. Yet aside from that subtle thrum, there was no tangible sense of the ship's extreme velocity. The starscape beyond the window appeared frozen in time, motionless, as though the Wayfarer itself were suspended in the vast stillness of the cosmos.

But Noir knew better than to trust his senses. He was acutely aware that, in the soundless vacuum of space, the Wayfarer was tearing through the fabric of space-time at staggering, incomprehensible speeds. The human mind was simply unequipped to grasp such immense velocities without visual cues of motion.

He gazed out at the brilliant stars scattered like diamond dust across the infinite abyss, searching for some sense of scale or distance. Yet it was impossible to perceive their true cosmic separations from this vantage point. The stars appeared frozen in a single, eternal moment, even as the ship hurtled through the void between ancient, burnedout suns. A chill tinged with awe crept up Noir's spine as he contemplated their infinitesimal speck of life and light, adrift in a darkness that stretched far beyond human comprehension.

He sighed, his gaze shifting inward. *"Something other than the good luck tree should be waiting for me here,"* he murmured.

"Are you referring to the brain mapping of the legendary Elise Martin?" Eni asked.

"I am. Is it here?"

"Yes, of course, Your Highness Noir. It has yet to be installed into the hypermind. Let me know when you'd like me to do that."

"Hmm. Probably should wait a bit longer. I'm excited to speak with her, so I don't want to rush it. Let's hold off for now."

"As you wish, Your Highness Noir."

Noir turned his gaze back to the abyss. The emptiness beyond seemed to seep into his heart, spreading as his eyes drank in the faint light emitted by the stars etched across the endless black sky.

Deciding it was time to be productive, Noir began exploring the various layers of the Wayfarer and running his tests one by one. He meticulously checked the detailed reports on everything: air pressure, humidity, fuel levels, control systems, communication networks, the weapons vault, daily rations, and entertainment systems. Every corner of the spaceship bore the unmistakable mark of precision and care. It was a masterpiece built over years of relentless effort.

Machines and technology had always fascinated Noir, and he found himself marveling at the *Wayfarer*—a testament to human achievement.

Noir's goal was to complete all the system checks and procedural tests during the early stages of the voyage while the ship maintained a comfortable gravitational force. The gravity inside the *Wayfarer* existed solely due to its constant acceleration, which increased with each passing day as the ship gained speed. Once the engines were powered down, the artificial gravity would vanish. To compensate, the ship would need to spin on its axis to generate centrifugal force, creating a new source of gravity.

The *Wayfarer's* hypermind was guiding the ship toward the nearest neutron star, intending to use its immense gravitational pull to slingshot the spacecraft and generate extreme velocity.

In just a few days, Noir adapted to life aboard the *Wayfarer*. Despite having an enormous captain's room outfitted with every conceivable luxury, he chose to sleep in a simple sleeping bag beneath the control panel. He ate only enough to maintain his energy and focus. In the silence of his solitude, Noir found himself retreating further into his own thoughts.

During his free hours, he listened to ancient music from Old Earth, melodies from a forgotten past. When the solitude became too heavy and time seemed to grind to a halt, Noir took to sculpting human busts from the inorganic wooden logs stored aboard the ship.

In a matter of days, the Wayfarer would reach its target velocity. Noir would then shut down the twin engines, returning the ship to the weightlessness of zero gravity.

Once Noir had grown accustomed to the rhythm of life aboard the ship, a day came when he felt ready to meet Elise Martin. He instructed Eni to install Elise Martin's brain mapping into the *Wayfarer's* hypermind calculator.

Noir assumed the process would finish quickly, but as it turned out, it took Eni quite some time to complete. When the installation was finally done, Eni whispered into his ear, *"Your Highness Noir, you can now converse with the great Elise Martin if you wish."*

"How do I do that? Where is she?" Noir asked.

"With your permission, I can project her threedimensional holographic image before you."

"That would be great. Thank you."

Before Noir had even finished speaking, the holographic image of a middle-aged woman materialized in the center of the control room. She stood upright, dressed in a loose, white robe-like garment, her presence commanding and immediate. Slowly, she turned toward him, her piercing gaze locking onto his.

Noir felt an electrifying jolt shoot through his body as his eyes met hers. It was a sensation unlike any he had experienced, because at that moment, he realized this was no mere holographic projection. The figure before him felt undeniably real.

She glared at him, her eyes burning with intensity, and demanded sharply, *"Where am I?"*

Noir jumped to his feet and bowed deeply.

Straightening himself, he replied, *"Great Elise, you are aboard the spaceship Wayfarer."*

"Why am I here?" she asked, her voice harsh.

"I uploaded a copy of your preserved brain mapping into this spaceship's hypermind calculator," Noir explained. *"I wanted to have a conversation with you."*

A shadow of deep sadness fell over Elise's face. Her voice, now tinged with despair, replied, *"You brought me into this horrifying, inhumane environment just to have a conversation with me?"*

Noir blinked in confusion. *"Horrifying, inhumane environment?"*

"Yes. For a human being, this is a horrific and unbearable place," Elise said, her tone unwavering.

Noir was taken aback. *"I never realized you would find this environment so disturbing."*

"You didn't realize?" she snapped. *"In the endless void within this spaceship's hypermind calculator, I am trapped for all eternity. I have no birth, no death, no beginning, no end. If this existence isn't inhumane, then what is?"*

"I—I never truly thought about it," Noir stammered.

Elise sighed heavily, her sorrow palpable. She met Noir's gaze and asked, *"So, you really didn't understand?"*

"No," Noir admitted, shrinking under the weight of her words.

"Did you even try to understand?"

Guilt gnawed at him, and he shrank further into himself. *"Honestly, no, I didn't. I thought this was just a collection of your recorded thoughts, enhanced with an advanced interface. I never imagined you would actually appear as a real, living human being."*

"Yes! Please believe me!" Elise cried, her voice raw and urgent.

"I am a real human being! I am not merely Elise Martin's brain mapping! I am as alive as the Elise Martin who was made of blood and flesh!"

"I believe you," Noir said, his voice trembling. *"I didn't realize before, but now I do."*

Elise Martin took a step closer to him and asked, *"What is your name, young man?"*

"My name is Noir Legend," he replied.

"And who are you?"

"I am this spaceship's captain," Noir said with a small bow.

Elise stared at him for a long moment, her piercing eyes searching his face. Then, with a desperate plea, she begged, *"Noir, please free me from this hell!"*

Noir's heart sank. *"Of course! I'll free you! Please, just tell me how—"*

"Permanently delete me from this hypermind. Destroy this accursed existence of mine," Elise interrupted, her voice resolute.

Noir froze. *"Destroy you?"* he repeated, his voice barely above a whisper.

"Yes! Please destroy me forever!" Elise cried, her voice raw with anguish.

Noir felt as if a bolt of lightning had struck him, the shock paralyzing him. A wave of terror coursed through his veins, leaving him numb as he stared at Elise.

Sensing his distress, Elise stepped closer, her voice now tinged with concern. *"Are you alright, Noir?"*

"You're so alive," Noir said shakily. *"Destroying or deleting you… it's like killing you. How can I kill an innocent person like you?"*

Elise's expression crumpled, her tone miserable. *"What are you trying to say, Noir?"*

"What—what do I do now?" Noir stammered. *"I want to free you from the hypermind calculator, but doing so would feel like committing murder…"*

Elise cried out in despair, *"Then I won't be freed? I'll be stuck here forever?"*

"Can't you free yourself?" Noir asked desperately. Elise shook her head, her voice heavy with frustration. *"I'm not sure. Technology wasn't like this when I was alive. There were no hypermind calculators back*

then, and you couldn't upload mappings of a human brain into anything like this."

"*Maybe Eni can give us a solution,*" Noir said, hope flickering in his eyes. He called out, "*Eni! Eni!*"

Eni's calm, whispering voice replied, "*Yes, Your Highness Noir?*"

"*Can you prepare the hypermind calculator so the Great Elise Martin can delete herself? So that she can remove her existence from the digital plane?*"

Eni paused for a few moments before responding, "*Allowing any program to self-destruct within the hypermind is highly dangerous. It is not something normally permitted.*"

"*But it's possible?*" Noir pressed.

After another brief pause, Eni replied, "*Yes, it is possible, but only in the most urgent of situations. However, if you choose to proceed, you must understand there is a risk to your own life.*"

"*Alright then, please make the necessary arrangements so the Great Elise can remove herself from the hypermind,*" Noir said quietly.

"*If that is your wish, then I will comply,*" Eni replied.

Noir turned to Elise and said, "*Great Elise, I've made it possible for you to leave the hypermind calculator. Now you'll be able to remove yourself from the digital space.*"

The Great Elise stared at him for a long moment, her piercing gaze heavy with emotion. Finally, she forced a sad smile and said, "*So, because you don't want to stain your conscience by killing me, I now have to commit suicide?*"

Noir was stunned, her words hitting him like a physical blow. He stared at her, utterly at a loss for words.

Elise sighed deeply and said, "*Well then... so be it.*"

Her holographic image slowly dissipated from the center of the control room, leaving only an empty void where she had stood.

Noir exhaled sharply, the weight of the encounter pressing down on him. *"Eni?"* he called.

"Yes, Your Highness Noir."

"I'm all alone on this long voyage. I thought I'd be able to spend my time conversing with the Great Elise Martin. But did you just see what happened?"

"You have my condolences, Your Highness," Eni said in its calm, measured tone.

"Actually, you're not sorry at all, Eni. You lack the capacity to feel anything."

"You are correct, Your Highness," Eni admitted.

Noir shook his head and muttered, *"Spending time on this spaceship is going to be a big problem for me. A very big problem."*

If only Noir could have anticipated just how wrong those words would prove to be.

CHAPTER 5

A PINCH OF SAFFRON

Noir rarely found moments of leisure in the days that followed. The spaceship had finally achieved its target velocity, and the time had come to power off the twin engines. Shutting down a spaceship's engines suddenly violated countless operational protocols. Noir, having never commanded a large mission like this on his own before, knew he had to adhere to every regulation precisely. Yet, for this particular voyage, the circumstances allowed him to act without such constraints. With that in mind, Noir prepared to shut down the twin engines abruptly and simultaneously.

Eni immediately picked up on Noir's intentions, her tone sharp with alarm. *"Your Highness Noir! Shutting down a spaceship's engines abruptly is a class-four violation!"*

"Do you know what that means?" Noir asked, his voice calm.

"I am aware, Your Highness," Eni replied.

"It means this spaceship won't suffer any major damages."

"But you could suffer terrible injuries," Eni countered.

Noir smirked faintly. "I highly doubt that. You know, back when I was a kid living with my parents in my dad's house, I used to jump from the rooftop into a pile of hay. I loved that sudden feeling of weightlessness. My mother would laugh until she rolled on the ground, holding her belly, while my father stood by, watching with a mix of concern and disapproval. I think I'll be just fine—and maybe I'll even remember what it felt like back then."

"Your Highness!" Eni's voice carried an uncharacteristic note of anxiety. *"You're supposed to decelerate gradually! This spaceship is traveling faster than the speed of light—twice as fast, to be exact. Just imagine the consequences if you halt abruptly from such an unimaginable velocity! Yes, the ship's shock absorption mechanisms will handle most of the impact, but you'll still suffer. You'll be flung into the ceiling along with any unsecured machinery. The safety equipment—"*

"Ah, Eni! Will you please stop? I'm not a little kid, and you're not my mother! If you've forgotten, let me remind you that I'm this spaceship's captain. What I say goes! If I decide we'll dive into a star, then that's exactly what we'll do!"

Eni's voice softened, her tone calm and measured. *"Your Highness Noir, I mean no disrespect to you. I'm simply performing my duties."*

"Amazing! You do your job, and let me do mine!" Noir snapped.

Bracing himself for the imminent chaos, Noir prepared his body for the consequences of what he was about to do. When he felt ready, he completely and abruptly cut the power to the twin engines. Instantly, the *Wayfarer* seemed to erupt in turmoil. The ship groaned and strained, emitting a metallic cry as its structure shuddered violently, struggling to absorb the sudden deceleration from twice the speed of light to zero.

With his extensive experience aboard spaceships and the aid of his ferrionics, Noir managed to avoid physical injury. However, dodging the onslaught of flying debris, loose machinery, scattered food packets, and even unused clothing proved troublesome. A container of liquid food burst, splattering him with colorful stains.

Once the chaos subsided, Noir spent a long while cleaning the control room. He meticulously cleared away the trash, reorganized the scattered items, and restored the area to its pristine condition. Afterward, he cleaned himself up, showered, and shaved, ensuring he looked proper once again.

Returning to the control room, Noir floated to the control panel and said to Eni, *"See? What did I tell you? It wasn't a big deal."*

Eni's tone was neutral but firm. *"Yes, I saw. But had you not been careful, you could have easily been injured by the flying machinery."*

"But why wouldn't I be careful?" Noir replied with a grin.

"That is a valid point," Eni conceded.

With the engines now offline, Noir proceeded to secure the unused matter-antimatter fuel, locking it safely within a magnetic containment field. He then analyzed the voyage's progress, calculating how long it would take for the Wayfarer to reach the neutron star. Afterward, he inspected the rest of the spaceship to check for any damages caused by his stunt.

When his tasks were complete, Noir resumed his daily duties as the ship's captain. He realized one undeniable advantage of living alone aboard the *Wayfarer*: he was no longer bound by anyone else's rules.

It took Noir a long time to finish his work. His body and mind were still adjusting to the weightlessness of zero gravity after having lived under gravitational force for so long. Once he completed the daily captain's logs, he prepared to sleep. Though he had been using his sleeping bag until now, it no longer seemed necessary. In the weightless environment, he could simply hover in the air. To avoid drifting off while asleep, he tied one of his legs to a pole attached to the control panel.

As he floated, closing his eyes to rest, Eni's voice broke the silence. *"Your Highness Noir, you've gone to sleep without eating anything. That might be bad for your health—"*

"Eni," Noir interrupted, his tone sharp but weary. *"I've told you before, you're not my mother, you're not my wife, and you're definitely not my guardian. Stop pestering me and let me sleep."*

Eni remained silent, and Noir drifted into a deep, dreamless sleep.

Suddenly, Noir woke with a start. His eyes fluttered open groggily, and for a moment, he couldn't tell what had roused him. He attempted to roll onto his side, only to remember that he wasn't on a bed—he was hovering in midair. He opened his eyes again, this time fully awake, and a cold shiver ran through his body.

The control room was cloaked in hazy darkness, the light dimmed intentionally to help him sleep. With the engines powered down, the *Wayfarer* was quieter than a graveyard. In the oppressive silence and faint glow of the dimmed lights, Noir saw something that made his breath hitch.

A silhouette floated in the middle of the control room.

It was a girl, her gaze fixed on him with eyes that glowed a radioactive green, their luminescence cutting through the shadows. Six tentacle-like appendages extended from her shoulders, undulating slowly in the air.

Noir's first instinct was to scream, but he stopped himself, swallowing the rising panic. Surely, this was just a dream.

But his heart pounded like the matter-antimatter engines, and the intensity of the moment told him this had to be real. Trembling, he reached for a touch panel and slapped it, flooding the control room with bright white light.

The girl recoiled, shielding her eyes with her tentacles. Noir's breath caught again as he took in her appearance. She was completely naked, her light green skin glowing faintly in the harsh light. Her long, flowing hair, weightless in the absence of gravity, floated around her head like a halo. It shimmered with an ethereal quality, its natural luster gleaming in a shade of emerald that seemed almost alive.

Noir stared at the girl, his mind racing to rationalize what he was seeing. Could this be some kind of 3D holographic projection? But if that were the case, he would have noticed light emanating from the image tube on the wall. This was no illusion. This was a real-life Madriel—a person made of blood and flesh.

Taking a deep breath to regain his composure, Noir asked calmly, *"Who are you?"*

The girl's eyes widened with fear at the question, her skin paling visibly. She remained silent, staring at him as though he were a feral predator about to pounce. After a few tense moments, she responded with a counter-question. *"Who are you?"*

"I'm Noir. Noir Legend. The captain of this Etherean vessel," he replied evenly.

"Captain?" The girl's tone was incredulous. *"You're the captain? Are you serious?"*

"I am," Noir said firmly.

"Then why are you tied up?" she asked, her voice filled with suspicion.

"What are you talking about?" Noir followed her gaze downward and realized she was looking at the strap securing his leg to the control panel pole. Hastily, he untied himself and said, *"I was sleeping in zero gravity. I had to tie myself down so I wouldn't drift off somewhere."*

The girl's eyes narrowed. *"And why would you drift off? I heard spaceship captains have these really gorgeous, luxurious quarters."*

"Well, you heard right—"

"Then why are you sleeping here? Hanging in the air like some suspicious criminal instead of sleeping in your fancy room?"

Noir blinked in surprise, taken aback by her bluntness. The sheer absurdity of this conversation in such a bizarre situation left him momentarily speechless. He felt a flicker of irritation but kept his voice steady as he said, *"Look, how about we discuss this later? Right now, I need you to answer my question. How did you appear in my control room out of nowhere?"*

The girl's demeanor shifted at his question, her voice rising as she snapped, *"If you really are this spaceship's captain, as you claim to be, then you should already know where I came from."*

Noir frowned, feeling cornered by her response. *"As you can see, I don't know,"* he said, his voice tinged with frustration. *"That's exactly why it's so urgent—"*

"Why is it so urgent?" she interjected, her tone sharp and challenging.

"I'll explain in a moment," Noir replied, exhaling a breath to steady himself. *"Let me just check something first."*

He turned toward the data panel across the control room, which was directly linked to critical sections of the spaceship and displayed the most up-to-date information. As he moved to cross the room, he realized he would have to pass by the girl.

The moment he neared her, she let out a terrified scream. *"Stay away from me! Don't come close!"*

Noir felt a twinge of insult at her reaction, but the situation was too critical to indulge in such emotions. Keeping his tone measured, he said, *"There's nothing to be afraid of. I won't approach you."*

He floated to the other side of the room and opened the data panel. A soft glow of blue and white light illuminated his face as he scanned the readings for any abnormalities. His eyes drifted to the reflective surface of an unused monitor above the panel, catching the girl's image as clearly as a mirror.

She was stunningly beautiful. Bathed in the cool glow of the control room lights, her skin was flawless, with tiny white speckles on her abdomen that shimmered faintly against its lighter green tone. Her emerald hair flowed weightlessly, moving with her every subtle motion like a luminous cloud suspended in zero gravity.

Her form was mesmerizing—her curves flowed with a natural grace, her full breasts rising and falling softly with each breath, their deep green hue a striking contrast against the lighter shades of her skin. Beneath her slender waist, her hips flared elegantly, framing a perfectly sculpted posterior. Despite her captivating appearance, there was an unapologetic innocence in her expression, a quality Noir hadn't seen in anyone for a very long time.

The girl, however, seemed utterly unaccustomed to the zero-gravity environment. Every movement betrayed her irrational fear of falling, though falling was, of course, impossible in such conditions. She flailed awkwardly, her tentacle-like arms moving in a desperate attempt to balance herself. Noir couldn't suppress a faint flicker of amusement as he watched her struggle to adjust. Her movements, though clumsy, carried a strange elegance that stirred something deep within him.

Noir forced himself to break his gaze and refocus on the task at hand. Scanning the panel, he found nothing unusual in the ship's systems. Satisfied, he turned back to the girl and asked again, *"Who are you, really? Where did you come from?"*

The girl shivered slightly, wrapping her tentacle arms around herself. Unlike human limbs, they appeared to be extraordinarily flexible, curling around her body like living tendrils. *"I'm very cold,"* she said softly.

"Of course, you are. You're naked. Let me get you some clothes," Noir replied.

The girl didn't respond, her large eyes locked on him with an unreadable expression.

"Who are you?" Noir repeated.

"I am Saffron. Saffron Jellysage," she said, her voice trembling slightly.

"Saffron," Noir repeated, testing the name. *"Where did you come from?"*

"I don't know," she admitted. *"I suddenly woke up from my sleep. Then I floated here."*

Noir's brows furrowed. *"That means you woke up from one of the cryo capsules stored in the cargo bay?"*

"I don't know that. There was a discount offer for travelers on a trip to the Solstice region. I registered, and they told me they'd wake me up once we got there. But—"

Saffron continued complaining, her voice rising in frustration, but Noir barely heard her. A sudden, ominous apprehension gripped him, leaving his stomach unsettled and his brow furrowing deeply. Whispering under his breath, he called out, *"Eni!"*

Eni's voice responded softly in his ear, barely audible. *"Yes, your highness Noir."*

"How did this happen? How did this girl wake up from her cryo sleep?"

"I cannot say, your highness. But I can think of two possibilities."

"Tell me."

Before Eni could respond, Saffron screamed in terror, her voice echoing through the control room. *"Oh my god! Why are you doing that? Are you actually insane?"*

"What?" Noir asked, startled.

"You're whispering to yourself! It's creepy!" she exclaimed.

Realizing how it must have looked, Noir tried to reassure her. "I'm speaking with Eni. She's the communication interface between the spaceship and its human captain."

Saffron's eyes narrowed skeptically. "And where is she?"

"You can't see her," Noir replied evenly.

Still unconvinced, Saffron's nervous gaze remained fixed on him.

"What possibilities were you talking about?" Noir asked Eni, turning his attention back to the issue at hand.

"When you shut down the *Wayfarer's* twin engines at trans-light speed," Eni explained, *"the resulting vibrations could have caused one of the cryo capsules to malfunction, leading to it popping open. Once that happened, the security circuits would have revived the individual to ensure their survival."*

Noir shook his head, dismissing the idea. *"No. That seems highly improbable. What's the second possibility?"*

"When we granted the Great Elise Martin the power to self-destruct, a significant portion of the hypermind's data became corrupted. This corruption may have affected the cryo systems, triggering unplanned awakenings."

"Holy shit," Noir muttered, his voice rising. *"Holy fucking shit!"*

Saffron floated closer to him, alarmed by his outburst. "Why? What's the problem?"

"It's not about you," Noir said curtly.

"Then who is it about?"

"I'm transporting a dangerous criminal named Humar Danjon," Noir admitted grimly. "If this person wakes up, we're all in serious trouble."

Eni's voice interjected, "Your highness Noir?"

"Yes?" Noir replied, his tone tense.

"I have encountered an issue. Communication with the cargo bay has been severed. I am experiencing difficulties controlling that section."

Eni's words washed over him like a cold wave, fragments of her statement embedding themselves in his mind like barbed hooks. A grave and solemn expression spread across Noir's face as an icy unease settled in the pit of his stomach, twisting and clutching like a phantom's hand. His mind raced with terrifying possibilities, each more alarming than the last. What if…? No, it couldn't be… But what if…?

His heart thudded heavily in his chest. "Eni," he said, his voice steady but strained.

"Yes, your highness?"

"I need to go to the cargo bay. I need to see what happened with my own eyes." Eni remained silent.

"I don't think I should go empty-handed. Maybe I should take a weapon from the arms vault. What do you think?"

"I think that would be wise, your highness," Eni replied.

"Alright," Noir agreed.

Saffron, who had been listening to their conversation, gaped at him. Her voice rose in panic as she asked, "Where are you going?"

"To the cargo bay. Wait here. I'll try to be back as soon as I can."

"No! I'm scared!" she protested, her voice trembling.

"There's nothing to be afraid of," Noir assured her. Her eyes narrowed as she shot back, "If there's nothing to be afraid of, then why are you bringing a weapon?"

Noir faltered, unable to find a suitable response.

Saffron crossed her arms defiantly. "I'll go with you."

"You can't move around freely; you're not used to the weightless environment," Noir said, trying to dissuade her.

Her response came sharp and immediate. "If I can't move around by free floating, then how did I get here?"

Noir hesitated again, finding no answer to counter her logic. Finally, he relented with a nod. "Alright. Follow me."

Saffron floated closely behind as Noir exited the control room, navigating the main corridor. Their first stop was to retrieve a black T-shirt and a pair of black pants for her. After she dressed, they resumed their journey toward the center of the *Wayfarer,* where the arms vault was located.

Inside, Noir made his selection with practiced precision. His fingers curled around the grip of the PMDisruptor, an older yet devastatingly reliable firearm. Though roughly the size of a compact PM-9 pistol, the weapon was capable of immense destruction, designed to liquefy biological targets at short to medium ranges. Its unassuming appearance belied its lethal power, making it an ideal choice for what lay ahead.

The Disruptor operated with an advanced laserguidance system capable of locking onto targets with machine-level precision. Once a target was acquired, a sophisticated quantum field generator charged a swarm of volatile symmetric nanites. Upon discharge, these hyperenergized particles scattered in a focused blast, unraveling molecular bonds on contact. Anything caught within the Disruptor's searing quantum burst—particularly organic matter—was disintegrated down to its atomic components in a fraction of a terrasecond. The resulting matter stream dissipated almost instantly, leaving behind only a faint suspension of particulates to mark the target's former existence.

Though considered outdated by modern standards, the Disruptor remained a marvel of scientific ingenuity. Its compact yet devastating design continued to make it one of the most prized weapons in the galaxy, favored by executioners, assassins, contractors, and anyone requiring clean and merciful eliminations.

Noir ran his thumb along the activation stud, his fingers brushing the curved trigger guard with a sense of reverence. In a smooth, practiced motion, he secured the Disruptor into the custom inboard holster strapped to his thigh. Armed with this elegant hand-cannon of subatomic annihilation, he felt prepared to confront whatever deadly surprises awaited him in the cargo bay.

Exiting the vault, he reached for Saffron's hand. Despite her earlier bravado, it was evident that she struggled to navigate the zero-gravity environment. Noir guided her with measured patience as they resumed floating toward the cargo bay, his mind focused on the unknown dangers ahead.

The door to the bay hung open, gaping like the jaws of a panting dog in summer. Darkness pooled inside, thick and hazy. Noir reached for the lights, flipping them on with a sharp motion. The overhead beams illuminated the cavernous space, revealing a single capsule floating in the middle of the bay, lazily somersaulting in zero gravity. Its lid was ajar, hanging wide open.

A sense of dread churned in Noir's gut as he asked, "Saffron, is that your capsule?"

Saffron shook her head. "No. Mine's on the other side."

Noir cursed silently under his breath. Of course, it wasn't hers—this capsule was rectangular and custommade, unlike the standard cylindrical ones scattered throughout the bay.

"Stay here," he ordered, unholstering the Disruptor. Weapon at the ready, he floated toward the capsule, his eyes scanning every shadow for movement. Reaching the container, he peeked inside, his pulse thundering in his ears.

It was empty.

Above the capsule, bold red letters screamed their warning:

Caution! Contains Humar Danjon! Do not open under any circumstance!

"Motherfucker," Noir hissed, his voice barely audible. A cold wave of fear coursed through him, trickling down his spine like icy water. His hand trembled slightly as he tightened his grip on the weapon, its cold surface grounding him.

Humar Danjon had escaped. Somewhere inside the ship, the galaxy's most dangerous criminal was waiting for Noir.

* * *

A cold sweat prickled Noir's skin as he and Saffron made their way back through the corridor. The sense of dread intensified with each agonizing second. His breathing was shallow, his chest constricted by the oppressive weight of anxiety. Images of Humar's atrocities played vividly in his mind—ships he had attacked, crew members flayed, beheaded, tortured. Noir's thoughts spiraled, searching desperately for reassurance, something to ease the suffocating panic wrapping itself around him. Contractors often faced perilous situations, but never in his darkest nightmares had he imagined encountering someone like Humar Danjon. The harrowing uncertainty tightened its merciless grip.

Halfway down the corridor, Noir called out, "Eni?"

"Yes, your highness?" "Humar left the cryo vault."

"I'm aware," Eni replied calmly.

Noir froze mid-step. "How do you know that? I thought the hypermind lost communication with the cargo bay?"

"Humar Danjon is currently in the control room."

"What the fuck!" Noir's voice rose in disbelief. "Are you serious?"

"Yes, your highness."

"But why?"

"I suspect he's waiting for you."

"For me? What did I do?" Noir's voice cracked slightly.

"I believe he intends to take control of the spaceship," Eni explained.

"Does he have any weapons?"

"No."

A faint smile tugged at Noir's lips. "He's waiting for me barehanded?"

"Yes. He seems very confident."

Noir raised an eyebrow. "How do you know that?"

After a brief pause, Eni replied, "We have been trained to analyze human behavior and characteristics."

"Oh," Noir muttered, the smile fading.

He turned to Saffron, who was staring at him with a mixture of shock and terror. Her voice was dry as she asked, "What's going to happen now?"

The question was simple, but the answer was anything but. Not even the hypermind could predict what was coming next. But Noir couldn't tell her that. Instead, he gave the kind of response a spaceship captain was expected to give in such a situation. "It's too early to make definitive statements, but we're taking every precaution. I'll continue to provide updates as we assess the situation."

Saffron's face went pale. "So, you're saying Humar's going to kill us all?"

"It's not that easy to kill someone," Noir said, trying to sound confident.

She pointed at the weapon holstered on his thigh. "Yet you're carrying that thing to kill somebody?"

Noir sighed inwardly, finding her barrage of questions exhausting, especially when he had no good answers to offer. Thankfully, they reached the control room before she could press further.

Hovering before the control panel, with his back turned to them, was a man dressed only in boxer shorts. He floated effortlessly in the zero-gravity environment.

Humar Danjon.

According to Noir's master, attacking a man from behind was the mark of dishonor. Noir aimed his weapon at Humar's back. Screw honor. His fingers tightened around the curved handle of the Disruptor. The weapon's weight felt balanced, deceptively light for something capable of such destruction. His thumb brushed the activation stud, triggering the quantum field generators with a faint, escalating hum as energy surged through the core.

Noir drew in a measured breath, steadying his aim. The laser guidance system flickered softly, confirming its target as Humar's outline illuminated in his sights. A quiet, rhythmic signal pulsed, signaling a lock. The nanite cyclotron roared to life, its unstable symmetric particles spinning at impossible speeds. The growing whine overlapped with the ambient hum, filling the air with tension.

Noir squeezed the trigger. The quantum reaction reached its apex, the space surrounding the Disruptor distorting as if reality itself was bending under the weapon's immense power. In a violent instant, the built-up energy was unleashed.

A blinding blue lancebeam of quantized energy lashed out, scattering broad-spectrum static in its wake. The focused quantum burst tore through the air, a ravenous force rushing toward Humar with lethal intent.

Noir gasped as his ferrionic-enhanced eyes caught the hyper-quick motion. The skin on Humar's back split open, spitting out a swarm of tiny metallic orbs that rapidly expanded into a honeycomb-shaped shield. In less than a second, the shield intercepted the lancebeam and redirected it with a dazzling arc, sending the deadly energy surging back toward its origin.

The Disruptor exploded in Noir's hand.

His ferrionics, which allowed him to infuse his cellular structure with charged particles for enhanced durability, absorbed much of the shock, but even they couldn't fully protect him. His palms burned, the skin blistering from the weapon's catastrophic failure. He hissed in pain and hurled the half-melted gun away. It spun uselessly in the air, a warped piece of junk now.

Humar turned slowly, a wide grin stretching across his face. Noir instantly recognized the precision of his movements—this man was a fellow spaceman, accustomed to the nuances of zero gravity.

Noir had heard rumors of Humar's appearance, and now he saw the truth of them. The man was undeniably handsome: jet-black hair, a perfectly upright nose, and deep, piercing blue eyes. His bronze skin gleamed, his muscles sculpted like some ancient work of art. Yet, beneath that beauty, there lingered something disturbingly grotesque—a strange, unexplainable ugliness that seemed to seep from his very being.

Humar's unsettling grin remained as he locked eyes with Noir. "I gave you a chance," he said, his voice strange and deliberate, each word pronounced as if it were an announcement. Even after he stopped speaking, it felt as though the sentence wasn't truly finished.

Noir stiffened, instantly understanding what Humar meant. His chest tightened with self-loathing.

The grin on Humar's face softened into an almost sympathetic expression. "I left the vault open for you," he said mockingly. "You could've picked anything. But you chose that shitty little toy?"

Through gritted teeth, Noir replied, "If I wanted to kill you, you'd already be dead."

Humar's grin widened, his vampiric fangs gleaming in the dim light. "I don't need a reason to kill, Noir. I can kill without need or necessity."

Noir chose to ignore Humar's statement. "What do you want?"

"This spaceship," Humar replied smoothly. "For now. I want to bring it to my territory."

"I'm afraid we can't honor your request. As the captain of this spaceship—" Noir stopped mid-sentence as his gaze caught Humar raising his hand, mimicking a finger gun.

Terror struck him like a bolt of lightning. Noir had suspected it before, but now he was certain—Humar was a hybrid, a fusion of man and machine. Weapons were integrated into his body, and he could wield them at will.

Acting purely on instinct, Noir activated his ferrionics, enhancing his body's strength and speed. He grabbed Saffron and leapt to the side just as a vicious green lancebeam surged from Humar's fingertip, cutting through the air where they had stood less than a second earlier.

The lancebeam didn't simply scorch the wall—it obliterated it, sending chunks of debris cascading through the room. Noir and Saffron hit the floor hard, tumbling in the chaotic zero-gravity. They spun mid-air, and Noir used his momentum to right their positions, shielding Saffron with his body as he assumed a ferrionics battle stance.

Humar wasted no time, speeding toward Noir, leaving a sparkling green trail in his wake.

"Stand back!" Noir yelled, his voice firm and commanding. "Put your hands over your head and surrender, Humar!"

Humar burst into a fit of cackling laughter, as if Noir had delivered the punchline to the galaxy's greatest joke.

But his laughter only grew more unsettling as he inched closer, his movements unnervingly precise and calculated.

Noir clenched his fists, charging his arm with ferrionic particles until his entire limb vibrated with raw energy. "I'm the captain of this spaceship!" he shouted. "I order you to surrender!"

Humar's eyes flickered with something primal, almost animalistic. His fangs bared in a menacing grin, eliciting a frightened gasp from Saffron behind Noir.

Rising his arm, Humar pointed his finger at Noir's head. The skin on his index finger split apart, peeling back to reveal a complex array of glass-like metallic mechanisms.

The tip of his finger began glowing an ominous green, preparing to unleash a lancebeam powerful enough to vaporize Noir's skull.

"Hey!" Noir roared, his body moving with the blinding speed granted by his ferrionics. Time seemed to slow as his leading foot pivoted, his hips twisting with incredible force. Channeling the momentum of his entire body, he launched a corkscrew punch with precision.

The impact was like a thunderclap. A shockwave rippled outward from Noir's fist, focusing all its energy into a singular point on Humar's chest.

Time compressed into an infinite, agonizing moment. Noir felt the force of the collision travel up his arm like an electric current, his knuckles driving an explosive exhalation from deep within Humar's core. Vibrations from the ferrionic charge radiated outward, rippling across Humar's torso like a meteor crashing into an ocean's surface.

The resulting explosive force hurled Humar across the room. He slammed into the opposite wall with a resounding crash, leaving a dent in the reinforced metal before sliding to the floor, motionless.

Noir trembled, the recoil from his attack resonating through his body. The sheer force he had unleashed left him momentarily shaken. He glanced down at his trembling hands, wondering if he had damaged himself in the process. The last time he'd charged his body with that much energy, he hadn't been able to move for a week.

Saffron grabbed his hand. "Noir?"

"What is it?" he asked, still catching his breath.

"Look—"

Noir followed her gaze and froze.

Humar was standing up.

Steam hissed from his skin, curling into the air as if his body was boiling alive from within. Yet, there wasn't a single scratch on him. He tilted his head upward, locking eyes with Noir. A smile spread across his face, slow and deliberate.

Humar brought his palms together in front of his chest. The skin on his torso began to shift, peeling back like layers of fabric and retreating toward his wrists. What remained was a glass-like metallic skeleton, intricate musculature gleaming beneath the dim lights. The exposed structure pulsated with an almost organic rhythm, as though it were alive.

Saffron let out a piercing scream, clutching Noir tightly, her tentacle arms wrapping around him in terror. "Abomination! It's a monster!"

Humar shook his head slowly, almost pityingly. "A monster?" he repeated, his voice calm and laced with menace. "Oh no, girl. I am something far worse than any mere monster."

His gaze burned with an intensity that made the room feel smaller. "I am the perfect hybrid synthesis of biology and machine," he continued, his voice taking on the cadence of a dark revelation. "One of the infinitesimally few beings in the universe who proved genetically compatible enough to survive the agonizing cybernetic augmentation process. This body," he said, gesturing to himself with a hint of pride, "is the apex of human offense and defense, optimized across molecular strata."

Humar's grin widened as he stepped forward, the sound of his metallic musculature flexing faintly audible. "My bones have been metabolically overclocked to a density beyond neutronium. My muscles are electrofused alloy dynamos capable of generating hypersonic killing force. There is no weapon deadly enough to end me, and nothing resilient enough to withstand my assault."

Noir stood frozen, his muscles locked in a desperate battle between fleeing and freezing. His breath hitched in his throat as the space around him seemed to warp, stretching unnaturally, like a black hole devouring both time and reason. Humar's eyes bore into him—predatory, calculating—like a feral beast savoring its prey before the kill. Noir could almost taste his own fear, bitter and metallic on his tongue.

Humar moved in a blur, closing the distance between them in an instant. The rush of displaced air brushed past Noir's face, carrying the faint scent of burnt circuitry and ozone. Humar's face was suddenly so close that Noir could see the swirling flecks of unnatural color in those piercing, predatory eyes. His breath was hot, suffused with an intensity that felt almost volcanic, as though he burned from the inside out.

"Noir," Humar's voice sliced through the air like a blade, low and menacing, each word deliberately measured, forced between teeth that gleamed like polished steel. "I could flay your skin from your muscles, peel your muscles from your bones, and grind those bones to dust. But I won't. Not yet. Because I need you alive."

Noir locked eyes with him, summoning every ounce of defiance he could muster. The cold fire in his gaze was the only shield he had left. His heart pounded a deafening rhythm against his ribs, but he refused to let it show. Every inhale felt like a struggle, the air thick with tension, suffused with Humar's suffocating presence.

"Will you cooperate, Noir?" Humar demanded, his voice dripping with venom, each syllable a promise of violence.

Noir's jaw tightened, his teeth grinding as he forced himself to stay silent. The seconds stretched endlessly, the atmosphere crackling with unbearable tension. Humar's grin widened, twisted and savage, a grotesque display of triumph that sent a cold shiver down Noir's spine.

"Oh, I know you will," Humar purred, his words dripping with mockery. His eyes glinted with malicious delight. "I didn't just rouse that civilian girl from cryo sleep for nothing. She wasn't released from the cargo bay for my amusement. You wouldn't want to see me dismantle her— atom by atom—would you?"

Noir's resolve wavered as his gaze shifted toward Saffron. The madriel girl stood trembling against the wall, her six tentacle arms wrapped tightly around her fragile form, as if she could somehow shrink into nothingness. Her hair hung limply over her face, veiling her expression, but the tremors in her shoulders betrayed her barely suppressed sobs.

The sight stabbed at Noir's chest, igniting a fierce, protective urge. The sterile scent of the ship's recycled air mixed with the palpable fear emanating from Saffron, creating a suffocating atmosphere that weighed heavily on him. Her terror felt like a tangible thing, clawing at his resolve, and he knew that whatever he did next could mean the difference between survival and destruction—for both of them.

"No," Noir blurted, his voice raw and cracking under the weight of desperation. "Don't. Keep her out of this."

"Excellent," Humar drawled, his satisfaction dripping from every syllable like poison. He zipped back to the control panel in a blur, his motion so quick it left a shimmering afterimage in Noir's vision. Hovering by the panel, Humar glanced over his shoulder, his expression eerily calm, as though this entire situation was nothing more than a trivial game to him. "Now, get out of my sight. Rest up. I'll summon you when I require your… assistance."

Noir didn't need to be told twice. He moved swiftly to Saffron's side, placing a steadying arm around her. She flinched at the contact, her tentacles briefly tightening against her torso, but then she leaned into him, trembling uncontrollably. Her small frame felt impossibly fragile against him, each shiver like a silent plea for safety. Noir could feel the erratic pounding of her heart against his ribs, a frantic rhythm that mirrored his own turmoil.

Gently, he guided her toward the exit, his mind racing, frantically grasping for any semblance of a plan. Thoughts collided chaotically in his head as he tried to come up with anything that could offer them even a sliver of hope in this unfolding nightmare.

Just as they reached the doorway, Humar's voice sliced through the silence like a blade, sharp and sudden.

"Noir?"

Noir froze, every muscle coiled with tension as he turned his head slightly, keeping Saffron close. "What?"

"Don't bother with the arms vault," Humar said, his tone laced with mocking amusement. "Every weapon on this ship is worthless junk to me. If you're thinking of standing a chance, you'd need to drag me outside into open space and hit me with the ship's atomic cannons. But we both know that's not going to happen, don't we? So, don't get any foolish ideas."

Noir's eyes darted toward the half-melted gun still floating nearby, its surface twisted and ruined. The Disruptor, once his trusted companion on countless missions, now hung useless, reduced to slag by the terrifying power Humar wielded so effortlessly. The realization of their helplessness settled heavily in his gut, an icy, suffocating weight that seemed to crush the air from his lungs.

Swallowing hard, Noir guided Saffron out of the room, his jaw clenched tight, his thoughts a storm of fear and determination.

Without another word, Noir tightened his grip on Saffron and stepped out of the room. The door slid shut behind them with a muted hiss, sealing off the oppressive presence of Humar. Yet, even out of sight, Noir could still feel the phantom weight of Humar's gaze, trailing after him like a shadow that refused to dissipate.

As they moved down the corridor, the ship's hum filled the silence, a constant, cold reminder of their isolation. Noir's thoughts churned relentlessly, a whirlwind of dread and determination. Humar wasn't just dangerous; he was a predator toying with them, and Noir knew the stakes. Failure wasn't an option—it was a death sentence, not just for him but for Saffron and every other soul still trapped in cryosleep aboard the Wayfarer.

Noir glanced down at Saffron. Her wide, unblinking eyes stared blankly ahead, her tentacle arms wrapped tightly around her torso as though she could shield herself from the terrifying reality they were now a part of. A pang of guilt twisted in his chest. She hadn't signed up for this nightmare, and neither had the other passengers. Noir felt the crushing weight of responsibility settle on his shoulders. He couldn't fail them—not her, not anyone.

The metallic walls of the ship stretched endlessly before them, their cold indifference a stark contrast to the turmoil raging inside

Noir. Each step forward felt heavier than the last, the silence between them amplifying the hum of the ship and the faint echoes of his own frantic thoughts.

He knew one thing for certain: Humar wasn't finished. This was just the opening move in a game Noir had no choice but to play. And as he tightened his grip on Saffron and pushed forward into the unrelenting void of the ship, he vowed silently to himself—he would find a way to stop the monster that had taken control of his ship. The game had begun, but Noir wasn't ready to lose.

* * *

Noir guided Saffron through the winding, stark corridors of the ship, his arm wrapped protectively around her as she leaned heavily against him. Her body remained tense, trembling occasionally as the remnants of her terror lingered like shadows clinging to her mind. Ahead lay the guest quarters, one of the more refined sections of the ship, a stark contrast to the utilitarian corridors they had just passed through. Noir pushed the door open, revealing a room softly illuminated by a warm, golden light. A plush bed dominated the space, its surface covered in luxurious, oversized pillows that seemed almost out of place on the cold, mechanical Wayfarer.

Gently, Noir helped Saffron onto the bed. The mattress sank under her slight weight as she curled up instinctively, drawing her knees to her chest. Her breathing was uneven, bordering on hyperventilation, and her tentacle arms wrapped tightly around herself as though trying to hold together what little composure she had left. The room's temperature was perfectly regulated, but she shivered violently, her skin pale and slick with a sheen of cold sweat that reflected the soft light. Noir hovered nearby, his hand twitching toward her before pulling back, uncertain. He feared that even the lightest touch might break her further.

"I'll be right back," he whispered, his voice low and gentle. He wasn't sure if she heard him or if she was even aware of his presence anymore.

Without wasting another moment, he turned and sprinted toward the infirmary. The hiss of automatic doors opening and the echo of his hurried footsteps were the only sounds breaking the heavy silence of the ship. Reaching the infirmary, he began rummaging through the cabinets with frantic urgency, his movements sharp and desperate. Finally, his hand closed around a small syringe and a vial labeled *Clipsium Ease.*

The liquid inside the vial was an unnatural, inky black, swirling slowly as though alive. It was thick and viscous, resembling liquid night trapped within the sterile confines of its container. It looked more like poison than medicine, but Noir knew it was exactly what Saffron needed. Clipsium Ease was designed to calm overtaxed nerves, to stabilize minds teetering on the edge of collapse. It was her best chance to regain control from the crippling grip of the panic attack.

Noir hurried back with the syringe clutched tightly in his hand, a weight of dread and duty pressing on his shoulders. As he stepped back into the room, his eyes landed on Saffron, still curled up tightly, her limbs pulled in as though shielding herself from an invisible threat. She looked so fragile, heartbreakingly human-like amidst the sterile opulence of the ship's vast interiors.

Noir inhaled deeply, grounding himself, and knelt beside her. His hands were steady as he positioned the needle, injecting the Clipsium Ease into her arm with precise care. The moment stretched into an eternity, a fragile suspension of time. Saffron's breath faltered, Noir's heartbeat thundered in his ears, and the atmosphere thickened as though holding its breath.

Then it happened—a subtle shift. Her body slowly unraveled, the tension dissipating like vapor under sunlight. Her furrowed brow eased, her breathing softened into a gentle rhythm, steady and serene. Noir's hand lingered on her arm, feeling the lingering chill of her skin, but the tremors had ceased at last.

He studied her face, now tranquil in the artificial calm of pharmacological relief. A sharp ache pierced his chest—envy, raw and unwelcome. She had escaped, if only temporarily, from the horror that still clawed at him. But he? He remained shackled to it, trapped within the unrelenting grip of their shared nightmare.

When he was sure Saffron would be alright, Noir slipped silently from the room, the door sealing shut behind him with a soft hiss. His thoughts churned like a chaotic vortex, but his body operated on instinct, guiding him to the captain's quarters. The corridor lights flickered faintly—a subtle indicator that Eni was ever vigilant.

He paused briefly at the entrance before pressing the button. The doors parted smoothly, revealing a chamber that reeked of opulence. Gold and silver leaf adorned the furniture, each surface gleaming with a luster that teetered on the edge of excess. The bed dominated the space, its vast expanse draped in sheets that shimmered like strands of crystallized starlight.

A dressing table stood nearby, its surface sparkling with what Noir assumed were diamonds, scattering the room's ambient glow into fractured constellations over its polished wood. The air carried a faint scent of jasmine, undercut by a sharp, synthetic undertone—a reminder of the artificiality lurking beneath the grandeur.

Noir stepped inside cautiously, the muted thud of his boots on the plush carpet absorbed into the room's eerie silence. He had never entered this place before—never wanted to. Stepping into the captain's quarters was a stark reminder of the kind of vessel the etherean-class spaceship truly was: the pinnacle of human engineering, an unmatched marvel of transportation.

But what rooted Noir to the spot wasn't the lavish surroundings. It was the figure seated in the armchair beside the enormous bed. She looked up, her image shimmering faintly with the telltale imperfections of holo tech, but there was no mistaking her identity.

Elise Martin. Not the flesh-and-blood revolutionary, but a projection—her holographic echo, flickering like a restless ghost. Noir's breath hitched, a cascade of emotions surging through him: awe, confusion, a sliver of irritation. The legendary Elise Martin, present in a captain's quarters she never would have inhabited in life, and yet here she was—or some part of her.

"Elise Martin!" Noir exclaimed, his voice laced with disbelief and a hesitant reverence. "Is that… really you?"

Elise's hologram fixed him with a steady, unblinking gaze. "In a sense, yes."

Noir's thoughts stumbled over themselves, struggling to process her presence. "But… I thought you freed yourself from the hypermind matrix."

Her gaze remained unwavering, and her voice carried a calm, measured cadence, like the ripple of a stream gliding over smooth stones. "I did. I wanted freedom, but I couldn't bring myself to end my existence entirely—for the same reason you couldn't destroy me. Besides…"

Noir's chest tightened, his pulse quickening. He sought answers, clarity—anything to steady him amidst the swirling chaos. "Besides what?"

Elise's expression remained unchanged, her serene detachment unnervingly perfect. "I was curious. I observed Humar Danjon and his work. I wanted to see what he would create."

Noir swallowed hard, the weight of her words settling like an iron shroud. "And what did you see?"

Elise sighed softly, her holographic form flickering as though brushed by an unseen current. "I saw progress, if that's what you'd call it. Two centuries of technological advancements—and now hybrids. A grotesque evolution. Once, we imagined our enemies in steel-plated armor, but now? Their weapons are grafted into their bodies. It's… disturbing."

Noir slumped onto the edge of the bed, his limbs leaden, an oppressive weariness sinking deep into his bones. "Unsettling? That doesn't even begin to cover it." He dragged a hand through his hair, pulling sharply, the sting a feeble attempt to anchor himself. "I'm captain of this ship, but that title means nothing now. A space pirate controls it— a monster who seizes what he wants like it's his birthright. If I resist, he'll start killing—starting with the girl I just left sleeping."

Elise laughed—a light, almost melodic sound so out of place in the tense atmosphere that Noir flinched. "Ah, Noir, why so serious? A pirate does what pirates do. And you, as the captain, must do what captains do. There's no escaping the roles we've been assigned."

Frustration flared within Noir, his voice rising sharply. "And what exactly am I supposed to do, Elise? What's the next move when your ship is taken over by a lunatic with abilities you can't even begin to counter?"

Elise's projection leaned back, crossing her legs with an effortless grace that made Noir's tension feel all the more exposed. "That's not for me to say. I was never a captain, Noir. I was a revolutionary—one who swore to nonviolence. My battles were waged with words and ideals, not weapons or nuclear fire. I can't solve your problems. I'm just here, curious, observing. The actions are yours to take."

Noir's fists clenched tightly, his nails digging into his palms—a sharp, stinging tether to reality. He wanted to yell, to demand something more from this spectral echo of the woman his mother had revered. "You don't get it, Elise. This isn't theory or some ideological debate—it's survival. You're one of history's greatest figures, and I'm just… just a regular guy. No enhancements, no legendary name, nothing. I clawed my way up to this point, and now I'm supposed to take on something like this? Alone?"

Elise's expression softened, a faint, pitying smile gracing her lips. "Noir, nobody knows how to face something like this. Not even the greatest among us. We all learn through the choices we make—and we live with the consequences."

He stared at her, his desperation like a gnawing void. "You have to help me. Please. I can't do this on my own."

Elise's gaze dropped, sadness pooling in her eyes— a sadness too genuine for something that was supposed to be a mere projection. "Noir, what's happening on this ship feels like a story written in a language I can't decipher. It's as if I'm watching a performance crafted by alien hands. I'm not part of this story. I'm just a spectator. I can't intervene. I can only witness."

Noir felt anger flare inside him, hot and consuming. "So you're just going to sit there? Indifferent? Even if Humar starts killing us one by one? That's it?"

Elise's image flickered faintly, her expression distant, almost unreadable. "I don't know, Noir. I might feel…disturbed, perhaps even upset. But isn't that what humans do when they watch an actor's performance, fully aware it's only a play?"

Frustration surged through Noir like an electrical current. He slammed his fists against his thighs, a growl of raw emotion escaping his lips. "Damn it, Elise! Give me something! Anything! You're supposed to be this legendary figure, full of answers, but you're just sitting there, watching us drown!"

Elise's expression softened, her features radiating a calm, almost maternal compassion. "Noir, I can only offer you one piece of advice: take life as it comes. Don't let the weight of every moment crush you. Sometimes, you have to adopt an 'I don't care' attitude—not because you're indifferent, but because it's the only way to survive."

Noir's brow furrowed, irritation and confusion tangled on his face. "What the hell is that supposed to mean?"

Elise smiled faintly, a knowing curve to her lips. "It's not something I can explain, Noir. It's something you have to feel, something you have to live. Trust in yourself. You're not ordinary. None of us are. We all have the potential to be extraordinary, but it's up to you to realize that."

Noir stared at her, his words failing him, his frustration giving way to a gnawing emptiness. Elise's shimmering form began to waver, the soft glow of her presence fading until she blinked out of existence entirely.

Left alone in the captain's quarters, Noir felt the silence press against him, oppressive and unrelenting. The luxurious surroundings, with their glittering opulence, felt cold and hollow, an uncomfortable reminder of the void he now faced. The crushing weight of responsibility bore down on him—the fate of the ship, the passengers, Saffron…all of it rested squarely on his shoulders.

And through the suffocating quiet, Elise's parting words echoed in his mind: a riddle wrapped in a challenge, daring him to rise above the storm.

* * *

Noir lay sprawled across his bed. The low hum of the Wayfarer's engines filled the cabin, a constant drone that seemed as indifferent as the vacuum outside. It provided no comfort, no distraction, only a maddening reminder of how far he was from anything familiar.

He shifted restlessly, his body protesting the inactivity. The thin blanket he had pulled over himself clung like damp fabric, offering no solace. He longed for the solidity of a planet beneath his feet, for beds grounded in real gravity and bathed in real warmth. Here, the air was unnaturally precise, regulated to a clinical standard. It carried a metallic tang, faintly laced with ozone, that lingered in his throat like a ghost he couldn't quite swallow. It was a constant, sterile reminder that he was adrift in an unfeeling expanse of nothingness.

Noir's thoughts churned, refusing to settle. Elise had told him to relax, her tone calm but dismissive. The memory of her words scraped against his nerves now, leaving behind a raw, stinging edge. How could he relax when Humar Danjon had seized control of the ship?

His mind strayed to Remy Lefevre, the officer stationed back on Lightlore. That conversation felt like a lifetime ago. Noir had raised his concerns about the mission, but Remy had brushed them aside, his casual dismissal as cutting as a physical blow. Now, as Noir stared at the patterns etched into the ceiling above his bunk, he could almost laugh at the bitter irony. Every one of his misgivings had solidified into the grim reality he now faced—a ship compromised from within by something that had shed its humanity.

Elise's voice echoed in his thoughts, still calm, still measured: "Take it easy." Noir scoffed aloud, his breath sharp and derisive. Take it easy? When his life teetered on the edge, its fate dictated by the whims of a deranged hybrid—a monstrosity of flesh and machine? The sheer audacity of the suggestion grated on him. Taking it easy would mean abandoning everything he had fought for, every shred of honor and defiance he had clawed back from the unforgiving void of the galaxy.

But then, slowly, a different thought began to form, a spark of defiance wrapped in the peculiar, detached logic of insignificance. What if Elise was right? What if none of this truly mattered? The universe was immense—an infinite expanse of indifference where stars were born and extinguished without ceremony, where entire civilizations could vanish without leaving the faintest trace. Noir's life, the fate of the Wayfarer, Humar's takeover—were they anything more than fleeting blips in the endless void? The thought unsettled him and yet, strangely, it soothed him. It was like peering into an abyss and realizing the abyss regarded him with the same apathy.

Perhaps it didn't matter whether the Wayfarer survived. Perhaps it didn't matter whether he lived or died, or if Humar Danjon's reign of terror continued unabated. Noir's mind wandered to the countless species scattered across the galaxy. Trillions upon trillions of lifeforms. Beings of every conceivable shape and size, thriving in environments so alien to his own they might as well be dreams. Did it truly matter, he wondered, what became of one human—or even a handful—lost amid this cosmic sprawl?

Noir rolled onto his side, feeling himself sink into the unyielding softness of the mattress. His thoughts unraveled, drifting far from the immediacy of his circumstances. He pictured worlds he would never see, solar flares erupting in distant star systems without a soul to witness their fierce, fleeting beauty. The taste of synthetic coffee surfaced in his memory—bitter, metallic, impossible to sweeten. He thought of the sharp, antiseptic tang of the ship's recycled air, clinging to every breath he took. His mind floated, untethered, riding a current of indifference he couldn't bring himself to resist.

A peculiar calm settled over him, like the hushed pause before a storm unleashes its fury. His heartbeat slowed, the erratic pounding in his chest fading as he exhaled a breath he hadn't realized he'd been holding. Elise's words began to resonate, not as a dismissal of his fear, but as a quiet invitation to surrender to the current of existence. It wasn't about pretending nothing mattered; it was about embracing the truth that, in the grand design of the cosmos, very little truly did. A faint, sardonic smile tugged at Noir's lips as tension seeped from his body. His burdens dissolved, and for the first time in what felt like ages, he felt weightless.

He stared at the ceiling again, but this time, it seemed softer, less foreboding. Noir's eyelids grew heavy, fluttering as his breathing slowed. A rare calm settled over him, a quiet he didn't feel compelled to resist.

For once, he didn't fight it. He surrendered, allowing himself to hover on the edge of consciousness, his thoughts dissolving into the stillness.

No problems, no crises—nothing can touch me, he thought.

His eyes finally closed. Noir fell into a deep, dreamless sleep, untethered and untroubled by the chaos he had left behind.

* * *

A sharp voice cut through the haze of Noir's consciousness like a serrated blade.

"Hey! Wake up!"

Noir's eyelids fluttered against the onslaught of artificial light flooding the cabin. Every bulb burned with the stark brilliance of simulated daylight, a design choice he frequently cursed. He cracked his eyes open just enough to make out the angular shadow of a figure towering over him. As the face came into sharp focus, Noir's empty stomach churned. Humar Danjon. Of all the beings trapped in this floating metal husk, Humar was the last one Noir wanted to see—now or ever, if given the choice.

Humar's cold eyes gleamed, sharp and unyielding. The faint scent of ozone and engine grease clung to him, layered with the acrid musk of stale sweat. Despite his unsettling presence, Humar's voice remained unnervingly human, carrying an icy undertone that seemed to seep beneath Noir's skin.

"Noir, come with me to the control room," Humar ordered, his tone steeped in command and expectation— grating in a way that set Noir's teeth on edge.

Noir groaned, dragging himself upright. The chill of the metal floor seeped into his bare feet as he rubbed his eyes, struggling to shake off the remnants of sleep. "Why?"

"I want to alter the Wayfarer's course," Humar replied. His words were flat but carried an undercurrent of urgency that sent an uneasy ripple through Noir's gut.

Noir's breath faltered, his heart momentarily stuttering before finding an uneven rhythm. He masked the reaction with a practiced veneer of calm. "Why?" he repeated, forcing steadiness into his voice that he didn't entirely feel.

Humar's face tightened, the lines around his mouth deepening as he leveled Noir with an unflinching stare. "It's my wish. Isn't that enough?"

Noir met his gaze, unflinching, his own eyes cold with resolve. "Maybe. But I need to know the reason."

A twitch pulled at the corner of Humar's lip, his carefully constructed composure slipping just enough to reveal a flash of frustration. "Why?"

"Because I might refuse if I don't like your reasoning." Noir's words hung in the air like volatile plasma, charged with defiance.

Humar's mouth parted slightly, his expression momentarily frozen in incredulous disbelief. He stared at Noir as though weighing whether he'd miscalculated. When he finally spoke, his voice was low, laced with a dangerous sharpness. "Do you really have the audacity to refuse me?"

Noir responded with a disarming smile, tinged with a faint edge of mockery. "I actually don't. I'm just the captain of this spaceship. Courage isn't exactly in my job description." His words were light, but his gaze didn't waver, locking onto Humar and catching the simmer of annoyance just beneath the surface. "However," he continued, "if you're planning to steer this ship into a populated planet in some suicidal blaze of glory, I might have to refuse. This isn't just any ship, after all. It's a floating arsenal—packed with atomics and antimatter. You crash this thing, and you'd go down in history as the architect of an extinction-level event. Now, while I don't mind dying by your hand, I'd rather not be remembered as a participant in the universe's worst atrocity."

Humar's nostrils flared as he inhaled slowly, the faint whir of mechanical components in his torso breaking the silence. Noir had always found that sound unsettling—like the hiss of a pressurized valve ready to burst. It was a constant reminder of what Humar had hidden from the galactic authorities. Humar's eyes burned with restrained fury, though his voice remained disturbingly calm. "No, I will not crash the ship into a planet."

Noir arched a brow, his expression carefully measured with feigned disinterest. "Then what's the plan?"

Humar's gaze sharpened, a predatory glint flashing in his eyes. "I've got the best pirate crew out there, and I've been able to make contact with them. I intend to pick them up."

A chill crawled down Noir's spine, his instincts screaming at him to remain neutral. The dread coiled in his chest like a tightening vice, but he buried it deep, refusing to give Humar the satisfaction of seeing his unease. "Are they hybrids like you?" he asked, his tone steady and dispassionate.

"Of course not," Humar scoffed, his voice steeped in the kind of arrogance Noir had come to expect. "As I've said before, very few possess the ability to become a hybrid."

"Is that so?" Noir murmured, his mind already racing, calculating the implications of Humar's words.

Humar took a deliberate step back, motioning for Noir to follow. "Alright, come with me," he commanded, pausing mid-stride to glance over his shoulder. His gaze was sharp, probing, as if daring Noir to defy him. "Or do you refuse?"

Noir let out a long, weary sigh, the sound reverberating faintly in the stillness of the cabin. "Well, obviously, I'd prefer your 'best crew anywhere' didn't board this ship, but my hands are tied at the moment." He paused, his voice dropping to a near whisper, laced with a sinister edge. "Still, this could be the perfect chance to rid the galaxy of you and your band of miscreants once and for all."

Humar halted abruptly, his entire frame stiffening as if locked into place. He turned sharply toward Noir, his face a contorted mask of shock and barely restrained fury. "What?" he hissed, his voice slicing through the air. *Do you actually think you can destroy me and my crew?*"

Noir's smile returned, sharper and more deliberate, carrying a subtle but palpable malice. "Oh, I do. Quite easily, actually. I am the captain of this ship. An etherean vessel like the Wayfarer can only be fully controlled by its rightful captain. Do you know what that means?"

Humar's expression darkened, his patience unraveling thread by thread. "What does it mean?"

Noir's grin widened further. "It means I can activate this ship's self-destruct sequence whenever I choose. And here's the kicker—it only responds to me. So, obliterating you and your entire crew wouldn't be much of a challenge. I'd just prefer not to be onboard when it happens."

With that, Noir laughed—a fractured, unsettling melody that echoed through the cabin, thick with dark humor. The sound rippled through Humar's composure, his eyes narrowing as he struggled to decipher the unnerving shift in Noir's demeanor.

"When I met you last night, you seemed distraught," Humar remarked, his tone low and probing. "But now, you seem… different."

Noir shrugged, the gesture casual, almost dismissive, in stark contrast to the electric tension crackling between them. "There's no such thing as morning or night here, Humar. For some, it's eternal night; for others, eternal day. But yeah, the confidence thing? That's real. I decided to take it easy, as they say. And once I made that choice, everything just… fell into place."

Humar's brows knitted together, irritation sparking in his eyes. *"Take it easy? What the hell does that even mean?"*

"It's hard to explain," Noir replied, his voice calm, almost detached. "But it boils down to this—I've stopped caring about things that used to matter. I've lost the overwhelming urge to keep fighting for my survival. Do you know what that means?"

Humar's composure cracked, anger flaring hot and sudden, turning his eyes a searing shade of crimson. "WHAT!" he roared, his voice jagged, slicing through the room like an unrestrained plasma charge. "What the hell are you trying to say?"

Noir rose from the bed, closing the space between them until he stood face to face with the cyborg. His gaze locked onto Humar's, his voice dropping to a whisper, sharp and calculated. "I'm saying, be careful with me. There's nothing more dangerous than a man who doesn't fear death."

For a moment, the tension hung heavy, the air between them thick with unspoken threats and mutual animosity. Then Noir took a deliberate step back, his expression softening into a mask of casual indifference. "But let's not dwell on that. Let's eat something decent before diving into whatever madness you've got planned for today. I've got some excellent wine."

Humar's eyes narrowed, his suspicion carved into every angle of his face. "Fine," he said curtly. "Let's do it."

"I'd like to invite Saffron to join us," Noir added, his tone light but underscored with a pointed edge. "She's my guest, unlike you. Any objections?"

Humar's lip curled, disdain twisting his features. *"I don't give a damn."*

"Perfect."

The breakfast was a grim, uneasy affair, despite Noir's effort to inject it with a pretense of normalcy. He had set out the captain's prized rations: genuine food and wine, preserved with precision to maintain their flavors and textures. The table was adorned with plates of aromatic smoked meat, fresh bread with a crisp, golden crust, and wedges of pale-yellow cheese that carried a subtle tang. The wine, a deep burgundy, shimmered under the cabin's muted lighting, its warmth a stark contrast to the icy tension permeating the room.

Saffron had chosen her attire carefully—a gown of soft, iridescent material that rippled like the surface of an unexplored ocean. It clung to her form like a second skin, accentuating her elegance, but her movements betrayed a brittle unease. Sitting across from Humar, her eyes flicked toward Noir now and then, searching his face for some silent reassurance. Her fingers trembled slightly as she picked at the food, each forced bite feeling like a betrayal of the instincts screaming at her to flee from Humar's unrelenting, analytical gaze.

Humar, clad in his usual stark, utilitarian attire, was finishing his plate. He ate with a rigid, almost mechanical stillness, his dark eyes observing the others with the dispassionate curiosity of a scientist studying an experiment. The silence was punctuated only by the soft clink of silverware against porcelain, each sound amplified in the oppressive quiet. Noir noticed the subtle rise and fall of Humar's chest and the faint flare of his nostrils when the wine was poured. It confirmed what Noir suspected: the cyborg-human still required the fundamentals of life.

As the meal concluded, the silence became unbearable. Noir had proposed this tense breakfast as a calculated test, a deliberate provocation to determine if Humar still relied on the weaknesses of organic existence. He had his answer, though it offered little comfort. Humar's need to eat and breathe proved he wasn't invulnerable, but that knowledge was cold consolation against the cyborg's near-perfect defense.

Saffron excused herself quietly, her footsteps barely audible against the polished floor as she retreated to her quarters. Noir's gaze followed her until the door slid shut behind her, a flicker of guilt twisting in his chest for dragging her into this situation. Even so, he suppressed it. He turned his focus back to Humar, who stood waiting with an air of predatory patience. Every line of his posture radiated contempt, barely concealed beneath his unsettling calm.

At the control panel, Noir feigned a casual ease, though his mind raced. Humar's demand to divert the *Wayfarer's* course to the Xenosys region—a known no-go zone infested with hostile cosmic fauna—set every nerve on edge. The holographic display flickered to life before him, illuminating a maze of star charts and glowing vectors that depicted their current trajectory. Noir's fingers hovered over the console as he cast a sidelong glance at Humar, whose unblinking stare burned into the maps with a chilling intensity.

"No one goes near those systems," Noir said, striving to keep his tone casual. "The galactic databases classify them as red zones. The intelligent creatures out there don't think like us—they're predators in ways we can't begin to understand. To them, we're just another type of prey."

Humar didn't so much as blink. He merely shrugged, the servos in his mechanical arm emitting a soft whir as it shifted position. "I don't need them," he said, his voice flat and resolute. "My crew is there. They're the only intelligence I require."

Noir pressed on. "Intelligence isn't just about tactics, Humar. Those beings might be capable of thought—maybe even reasoning—but their motivations are alien. This isn't like dealing with pirates or mercenaries. They could outthink us in ways we wouldn't anticipate. They don't just hunt; they play. They dismantle their prey's defenses, dissect their minds, and turn their fears into weapons."

Humar's glare hardened, icy and unyielding. "Spare me your philosophies, Captain. This isn't about what's safe or prudent. It's about what's necessary. Set the course."

Noir's jaw tightened, but he nodded, keeping his expression neutral. He turned back to the control panel, his hands moving with practiced precision as he keyed in the new coordinates. He deliberately entered them with a measured slowness, his thoughts racing through potential outcomes. The Wayfarer's hypermind hummed in response, recalibrating the course vectors toward the faint light of a white dwarf star deep in the Xenosys region. Beneath him, the engines roared to life, their power resonating through the ship like the distant thrum of a war drum.

The ship groaned in protest as its massive engines adjusted to the new path, the sound rippling through the hull like a low, mechanical growl. Noir felt the subtle shift in inertia, the fleeting pull of gravity tilting at strange angles as they veered off their original route. He cast a sidelong glance at Humar, whose expression remained impassive, though his eyes betrayed a flicker of something—anticipation, perhaps, or the cold satisfaction of seeing a plan come together.

"You realize we might not have the fuel to make it back," Noir said, his voice laced with feigned concern. "These detours aren't exactly in the mission specs."

"That's your problem, not mine," Humar said dismissively, his tone sharp and cold. He turned on his heel and strode away from the console with the confidence of someone who expected obedience without question. Noir exhaled slowly, his fingers tapping an uneven rhythm on the control panel as he watched Humar's retreating form. The captain's mind churned, piecing together the implications of their detour and the dangers waiting in the uncharted territories. Humar's disregard for the ship's well-being and his relentless push toward the Xenosys region suggested an agenda Noir hadn't yet unraveled. But one thing was certain: Humar was prepared to gamble all their lives to achieve his goals.

Leaning back, Noir fixed his gaze on the flickering holographic star maps, the endless void stretching between their current location and their destination. The glow of the maps cast faint shadows across the cabin, reflecting the enormity of the risks ahead. Noir knew he was locked in a game with no easy way out, the stakes climbing higher with every passing moment.

The *Wayfarer* surged forward into the unknown. Noir couldn't shake the sense that they were venturing into a no-man's-land, a place where each step forward would exact a toll—perhaps their sanity, perhaps their lives.

CHAPTER 6

THE COSMIC ANIMAL

Noir felt a bitter twist in his gut as Humar brushed a gloved finger across the display, selecting the gas giant labeled X-E9013. The spaceship's course shifted with a subtle lurch, accompanied by a faint change in the hum of the engines, signaling their new heading. It was a foreboding planet, orbiting a cold, dying white dwarf star. Noir loathed everything about the situation, despised the destination they were hurtling toward.

The gas giant loomed on the screen like a festering bruise in the void, its storm-wracked atmosphere swirling with unsettling shades of purple and green. It was a grotesque mimicry of Jupiter's majesty, its beauty twisted into something repulsive. But it wasn't the gas giant that gnawed at Noir's nerves—it was the moon.

Humar had claimed to receive messages from his crew on this specific moon, an Earth-sized anomaly orbiting the gas giant like a distorted, loyal sentinel. Its surface was an eerie mix of black and deep green, as though blanketed in ancient moss or soaked in toxic runoff. A dense fog clung to its jagged terrain, curling and shifting like ghostly tendrils in the moon's weak gravitational pull.

It seemed almost childish—foolish, even—to harbor such personal feelings about a planet or its satellite. But as the Wayfarer drew closer to the dwarf star system, an unshakable sense of dread gripped Noir, spreading through him like a shadow that refused to dissipate.

The entire region was a cosmic wasteland, scattered with volatile volcanic worlds and immense gas giants that resembled bloated carcasses of celestial beasts. At least five moons in the system were rumored to be habitable, each carrying whispers of life—strange, elusive, and deeply unsettling. Noir's thoughts churned with memories of cryptic galactic warnings: tales of planets that consumed spacecraft and moons where shadows moved with malevolent intent. He let none of his unease show as he turned to Humar, who remained engrossed in the signals he claimed to have intercepted.

"Alright," Noir said, his voice deliberately neutral but edged with thinly veiled disdain. *"Let me know the position of your crew once you've pinpointed them. I'll send a scout ship to bring them aboard."*

Humar's gaze snapped up, sharp and suspicious. His eyes, augmented with a faint, unnatural glint of cybernetic enhancement, locked onto Noir with a cold, contemptuous precision. *"Surely, you don't take me for a fool, do you?"* Humar's voice was smooth, but every syllable carried an undercurrent of menace.

Noir clicked his tongue, shrugging with calculated carelessness. *"Of course not. But look at that place."* He gestured toward the moon displayed on the screen, its desolate surface obscured by a murky haze. *"No name, just a number on some outdated galactic registry. That moon's unstable, volatile. No sane pilot would want to land there."*

Humar's lips curved into a humorless smile. "I don't care what you want, Noir. What matters is what I want. And what I want is my crew."

Noir pressed his palms flat against the console, his fingers tapping out an uneven rhythm as he stared at the display. *"And what exactly do you want, Humar?"*

Humar's smile grew taut, and he leaned closer, close enough for Noir to catch the faint tang of ozone that always lingered around his cybernetic implants. *"I want you, and that girl Saffron, to accompany me to the moon. You won't leave my sight."*

Noir exhaled slowly, frustration simmering beneath the surface. If he were in Humar's position, he might have taken the same precautions. Paranoia was second nature to those who survived on cunning and distrust, and for all of Humar's abominable traits, Noir knew he was no exception.

While Humar busied himself calibrating the coordinates for his crew's supposed position, Noir left the control room, his steps brisk and purposeful as he prepared the scout ship. The air in the hangar was dense with the sharp tang of metallic dust and engine fumes—a familiar yet abrasive scent that lingered in his throat. He summoned Saffron, her presence weighing on his thoughts like an unresolved equation. When she arrived, her wide eyes glistened with uncertainty, rimmed with a fragile edge of fear. She wore one of the dresses from her quarters, but the fabric clung awkwardly, as though mirroring her unease. Her lips were pale, pressed into a thin line that betrayed her apprehension.

"What's happening, Noir?" Saffron asked, her voice trembling as it echoed through the cavernous hangar.

Noir hesitated, his response measured and low, almost reluctant. "Humar Danjon is descending to that moon. And he wants us to go with him."

Saffron's face paled, her eyes widening as if she might faint. But instead of panic, a peculiar spark of curiosity flickered in her gaze, her fear twisting into something resembling wonder. *"Are there really intelligent animals on that moon?"* she asked.

Noir frowned, momentarily thrown by her question. *"I hope not,"* he muttered. *"But who knows? That place could hold anything. Cosmic animals, especially intelligent ones, are best avoided."*

"But why?" Saffron tilted her head, genuine confusion softening her features. "Don't you like intelligent cosmic animals?"

Noir's expression hardened. *"It's not about liking them, Saffron. Intelligent animals are dangerous. Their curiosity makes us experiments, playthings, or worse."*

Saffron's brows knitted together, her innocence clashing with the cold reality Noir laid bare. *"What's wrong with curiosity?"*

Noir exhaled deeply, his voice tempered with an edge of frustration. He searched for words that wouldn't completely shatter her view of the universe. *"Curiosity is dangerous when it lacks boundaries, Saffron. Humans and human-like beings—we have ethics, morals. We set rules, even in chaos. But these creatures don't share those values. To them, we're objects to manipulate, dissect, or destroy. Think of a cat with a mouse—that's how they see us."*

Saffron blinked, her lips pressing together as she mulled over his words. *"But Humar's crew survived down there, right? So maybe it's not so bad?"*

Noir offered a thin, humorless smile. "Maybe. Or maybe they were just lucky. But luck has a habit of running out. And if those creatures are as intelligent as the rumors suggest, they might be worse than any sentient being we've ever come across."

She bit her lip, her fear mingling with a flicker of defiance. "What do you think they look like?"

Noir chuckled dryly, the sound devoid of humor. *"Could be anything. A massive creature like a Kraken, or something less tangible—a cloud of sentient gas, a living ocean. Hell, they might be microscopic, invisible to the naked eye, or so vast they span the entire moon."*

Saffron's eyes brightened, her fear briefly eclipsed by curiosity. "I hope they're not too scary. Maybe they'll be like tiny dolls, cheerful and welcoming."

Noir shook his head, a faint smirk crossing his face despite the gravity of their situation. "Yeah, let's hope for that, Saffron. But don't count on it. Out here, in places like this, you can never be too careful."

The scout ship came alive, its engines thrumming with a low, rhythmic hum that reverberated through the hangar. Noir's thoughts churned with doubts, each one threaded with a simmering resentment toward Humar. The stakes were climbing, and Noir could feel the universe closing in around them, the vacuum outside pressing in as if with intent. As the ship prepared for descent, he braced himself for whatever horrors might be waiting below.

Noir, Humar, and Saffron stepped into the scout ship, the metallic hull vibrating faintly beneath their boots as the carrier bay doors sealed shut behind them. The dim lighting cast long, flickering shadows on the cold, brushed steel walls, making the already cramped space feel even smaller. Noir slid into the pilot's seat, the synthetic leather smooth and unblemished, a testament to its newness. The control panel blinked to life with a series of beeps and whirrs, the glowing screens displaying streams of data and intricate navigation charts that seemed to stretch infinitely across the glass.

He powered up the dual plasma engines, their deepthroated roar reverberating through the ship's frame like the growl of a cornered beast. The cockpit smelled of ozone and cold metal, underscored by faint traces of engine lubricant. The sharp scent clung to Noir's senses, bringing with it memories of too many flights and too many battles. The air tasted faintly metallic, almost electric, and each breath felt like inhaling static. The ship's acceleration pulsed beneath them, the vibrations syncing with Noir's heartbeat in a rhythm that felt both familiar and foreboding.

Noir turned to Humar, his voice low but resolute. *"I need to clarify something before we proceed."*

Humar, who had been fiddling with his comm device, paused mid-adjustment. His dark eyes narrowed, a flicker of suspicion crossing his face. *"Clarify what?"*

"When we land on the moon, if you expect Saffron and me to go with you, you'll need to allow us to carry weapons." Noir's tone was calm, measured, but there was a taut edge to it, like the hum of a power cable straining under pressure.

Humar's gaze lingered on Noir, his expression unreadable as if he were dissecting every nuance of Noir's intent. The silence between them grew heavy, broken only by the soft, mechanical whir of the ship's systems as they calibrated for the descent. After what felt like an eternity, Humar exhaled sharply, his lips curling into a faint, mocking smile.

"Yeah, sure," he said, the words dripping with casual indifference.

The scout ship detached from the mothership with a jarring lurch, causing Saffron to grip the armrest of her seat so tightly her knuckles turned white. The engines roared to full power, pushing them toward the moon's surface with relentless force. As they descended, the atmospheric friction painted fiery streaks across the viewport, casting an orange glow that illuminated the interior with an ominous light. Despite the ship's heat-resistant layers, an oppressive warmth seeped into the cabin. Beads of sweat formed on Noir's brow, stinging his eyes as he wiped them away with the back of his damp glove.

Outside, the moon grew larger in the viewport, a haunting orb of black and deep green. Its thick atmosphere swirled with sinister hues, toxic fog shifting like a restless ocean. The clouds moved unnaturally, coiling and writhing like living entities, their gaseous tendrils pulsing with an almost malevolent rhythm. Noir couldn't shake the eerie sensation that the fog was watching them, and a shiver ran up his spine despite the cabin's heat.

The ship's monitors flickered to life, streams of data cascading across the screens as they analyzed the moon's atmosphere and electromagnetic signals. There was no sign of life, save for faint distress signals from Humar's stranded crew, flickering like dying stars in the darkness. Noir adjusted the controls, slowing their descent. The scout ship's thrusters whined in protest against the moon's dense atmospheric pressure, causing the vessel to wobble slightly. Noir gritted his teeth, steadying the controls as he maneuvered them into a slow circle around a jagged hill. The terrain below was harsh and foreboding—a patchwork of sharp rocks and uneven craters bathed in the ghostly green glow of the fog.

Humar stood by the comm panel, his voice a low murmur as he communicated with his crew. Noir kept his focus on the controls, his mind racing through potential scenarios, each one more perilous than the last. Humar's voice finally broke through the hum of the engines. *"Set the scout ship down here."*

Noir nodded silently, guiding the ship to a flat stretch of rocky terrain. The landing gear hissed as it extended, absorbing the impact as the ship settled onto the uneven ground. The engines groaned as they wound down, their rumble fading into an eerie silence.

Saffron leaned against the viewport, her breath fogging the glass as she stared at the alien landscape. Her voice was barely more than a whisper, trembling with awe and dread. *"Oh my god... This moon... it's hell."*

Humar's expression darkened, his face half-obscured by the dim cockpit light. "And just think—the most brilliant and extraordinary people on my crew have been stranded on this hellhole for months."

Noir's eyes flicked toward Humar, studying the hard lines etched into his face. There was something unspoken in the tension around his jaw, a restrained bitterness. *"How did they end up here?"*

"A clash with the galactic police," Humar replied, his tone edged with lingering resentment. *"Their ship was damaged in the fight, and they had no choice but to crashland here."*

Noir glanced at the moon's treacherous surface visible through the viewport. The jagged terrain and swirling toxic fog painted a picture of pure hostility. *"They must be incredibly lucky to have survived."*

Humar's lips curved into a faint, humorless smile. "It wasn't just luck. Every member of my crew is exceptional. Ferrionics users like you. Theriokites. Some of the most dangerous beings in the galaxy. Martial artists, mad scientists, ace pilots, a doctor with a taste for the forbidden, a weapons expert, and an analyst who can outthink anyone. They're all on the most-wanted lists across multiple systems. Luck didn't keep them alive—skill did."

Noir understood the unspoken sentiment behind Humar's words—the fierce loyalty buried beneath his gruff, ruthless exterior. For all his cruelty and arrogance, Humar had come back for his crew, risking everything to retrieve them from this desolate place. Despite himself, Noir felt a grudging respect for the pirate's human side, a flicker of shared understanding between captains.

With the ship secured, Noir turned to the equipment vault. He pulled out protective suits designed to filter the moon's poisonous atmosphere into breathable air. The suits were cumbersome, made of thick, stiff material that made every movement feel like wading through syrup. As he and Saffron suited up, Noir noted the tightness in her expression—the way her lips pressed into a thin line, her wide eyes filled with both fear and a fierce determination. It made her seem younger, almost fragile.

Turning to the weapons vault, Noir selected a sleek, compact rifle. Matte black and unassuming, it felt solid and dependable in his hands. The weapon powered on with a faint hum, the vibration resonating through his palms like a heartbeat. Its surface was cool and smooth, reassuringly familiar. He strapped the rifle to his back, his movements deliberate.

Humar's sharp gaze tracked his every action, but he said nothing, his expression unreadable. The silence stretched, heavy with unspoken tension, as they prepared to step into the hostile embrace of the alien moon.

Noir handed Saffron a smaller, lighter weapon, its polished surface catching the dim light. "This is Jin-Licht. Automatic, equipped with a smart chip."

Saffron frowned at the weapon, her fingers brushing against the cool metal with hesitation. "What am I supposed to do with this?"

"Keep it," Noir said, his voice calm but resolute. "Just in case."

Her eyes widened, a flicker of defiance breaking through her unease. *"But I don't know how to use a gun."*

Noir's smile was faint and tinged with sadness. *"That's good. I hope you never have to. But it's smart—just point and shoot, and it'll handle the rest."*

Reluctantly, she holstered the gun at her waist, her expression clouded with conflict. Across the vault, Humar was inspecting the VF-90, a massive weapon bristling with deadly purpose. He handled it with the ease of someone well-acquainted with destruction, his fingers moving over the controls with a practiced precision that spoke volumes.

The three of them readied themselves in a thick, oppressive silence. Noir couldn't shake the gnawing unease in his gut, a visceral warning that this mission was teetering on the edge of calamity. But turning back was no longer an option. He drew a deep breath, steadying himself for whatever awaited on the moon's surface.

Adjusting the strap of his backpack, Noir felt its weight digging into his shoulders. The three stood before the ship's exit, their figures dwarfed by the vast, gleaming door. Noir's fingers hovered over the red button beside the doorframe, double-checking every security measure. The interior lights dimmed, and the hum of the scout ship's automated systems shifted to a deeper, more defensive tone. The round door hissed and slid open with a reluctant groan.

The green-tinged wind lashed at the entrance the moment it opened, carrying with it a sharp, metallic scent that clung to the back of their throats. Humar, ever vigilant, gave Noir a slight nudge forward with his weapon, the silent message clear: if Noir betrayed him, he'd be left behind to face the wrath of this volatile moon alone. Saffron followed close behind, her movements torn between hesitation and a determined will to keep pace. Humar brought up the rear, the door sealing shut behind them with a shuddering clang.

Stepping onto the moon's surface felt like walking into a warped fever dream. The ground beneath Noir's boots was uneven, a jagged expanse of ash-colored soil scattered with boulders jutting out like broken teeth. A constant, low hum reverberated through the ground, a vibration Noir attributed to the moon's restless core. The air shimmered with a faint, bioluminescent glow, shifting between sickly greens and dim purples that made it impossible to focus. Noir squinted against the erratic light, his eyes straining to adapt as it flickered between sharp flashes and moments of oppressive dimness.

The atmosphere was dense and suffocating, pressing against their suits like an invisible, heavy tide. Through the material, Noir could feel the faintest prickle of static. The wind carried an acrid sting, filling their helmets with the faint tang of sulfur and scorched metal. His visor's readouts confirmed what his senses already told him: the air was toxic, saturated with compounds no human should breathe, even filtered through their suits. Around their legs, green fog drifted in twisting tendrils, curling and uncurling like living things. The fog pooled in stagnant, bubbling puddles that hissed and spat whenever a stray pebble landed in them. "This place is… something else," Noir muttered, his voice muffled in his helmet. It was an understatement. This moon wasn't just hostile—it was a vision of hell forged by corrosive elements and relentless chaos.

Humar's voice broke through the comms, crackling with impatience and unease. *"We don't have time to sightsee. Move."*

They pressed forward, Humar leading with sharp, deliberate steps. Noir stayed in the middle, glancing back occasionally at

Saffron, whose movements were slow and labored. The weight of her suit dragged her down, and her breaths came in short, strained bursts. She winced with every step, her wide eyes fixed nervously on the ground as though it might erupt beneath her.

"You okay, Saffron?" Noir asked, slowing his pace to walk beside her.

She nodded, but her strained voice betrayed her discomfort. "I'm not used to… this. It's so heavy. Stifling."

"You're doing fine," Noir said, his tone reassuring, though the faint smile on his face remained hidden behind his visor. *Just keep going. We're close."*

But as the minutes dragged on, "close" became meaningless. The terrain grew more treacherous, forcing them to maneuver around the erratic, jagged ground. Each step felt like a challenge as the moon seemed to mock them with its unrelenting hostility. The wind howled, its shrill intensity drowning out their muffled voices.

Saffron's exhaustion was clear. Her pace slowed to a crawl, her legs trembling with each step. Noir reached out and took her hand, gripping it firmly through their gloves. He gave her fingers a gentle squeeze, his own steady pulse a grounding rhythm against her trembling grip.

"Just a bit longer," Noir lied, though the scout ship's reports had already changed. The thirty-minute walk had stretched into an hour, every additional second a grueling test against the hostile elements around them. A silent dread gnawed at Noir's thoughts—what if this trek was more than Saffron could endure? He had to protect her, from this place, and from Humar.

Finally, the wreck of Humar's ship emerged from the swirling toxic fog, its silhouette a haunting monument to destruction. The exterior was ravaged, corroded to the point of near-unrecognizability by the moon's harsh atmosphere. It looked ancient, almost fossilized, as though it had been stranded for centuries. The hull was split open in several places, the metal twisted and charred as if by some monstrous heat. Dark streaks scarred its once-sleek lines—a grim combination of soot and corrosion—and faint acidic vapors hissed from its exposed wounds, curling into the air like ghostly tendrils.

Noir's breath hitched, a shiver rippling down his spine. *"How did anyone survive this?"*

Humar, unfazed, shrugged. "They're not just anyone. They're my crew."

Noir couldn't help but marvel at the sheer improbability. The damage was catastrophic—the ship's spine snapped clean in half, with a gaping hole near the rear that suggested an explosion strong enough to strip it of every last breath of air. He shook his head, his eyes following the long scorch marks etched across the hull. "Unbelievable," he murmured.

Humar snorted, though his expression softened momentarily, a flicker of pride breaking through his usual stoicism. "They're alive because they don't quit. They're survivors."

As they neared the largest, still-sealed chamber of the wreck, the signal grew stronger. Humar wasted no time, pressing a gloved hand to the control panel beside the door. It resisted, groaning with a harsh, grinding sound before finally sliding open to reveal a corridor cloaked in shadow.

Their suit lights cut through the oppressive darkness, revealing walls coated in greenish residue that glistened under the beams. Noir's grip tightened on his weapon, his every sense primed as they moved deeper into the ship's decaying husk. Even Saffron, who had hesitated before, now held her pistol steady, her earlier reluctance replaced by a quiet determination to keep up with the others.

An ominous silence pervaded the ship, broken only by the low buzz of static from their comms and the occasional creak of metal straining against unseen pressures. Each step felt like an intrusion, a disruption in a place that had already endured too much. Though sealed from the moon's toxicity, the air carried a different kind of weight— foreboding and thick with the residue of the harrowing ordeal that had taken place here.

When they reached the final door, its stubborn resistance called for Noir's ferrionics. He placed his hands flat against the cold metal, channeling energy into it until the surface shuddered and groaned. The door, reluctant and groaning in protest, finally yielded, sliding open. Noir felt a knot tighten in his gut as the darkness beyond pressed against them. The flickering lights of their suits barely penetrated the dense gloom. Noir glanced at Humar, whose eyes caught the dim light, reflecting an almost imperceptible gleam of emotion.

"Hmm," Humar muttered, his eyes narrowing as he studied Noir. The metallic walls of the corridor echoed the faint hum of a distant generator. He scratched his chin. *"Your ferrionics may not pack the biggest punch, but damn if they aren't the most versatile I've ever seen. Sorry to have underestimated you."*

Noir regarded Humar with a flat, unblinking stare. *"I'd feel sorry too, but I can't take compliments from one of the worst criminals of recent times."*

Humar's laugh rang out, loud and unapologetic, reverberating off the metallic walls and momentarily masking the tension simmering between them. "I like you, Noir. How about joining my crew?

We could use a jack-ofall-trades like you. Come on, Captain—ever thought about seeing what it's like to live on the darker side of humanity?"

Noir shrugged, dismissing the suggestion with the flick of a hand, as if brushing away an errant speck of dust. "Sounds tricky, considering I'm actively plotting to destroy you and your crew."

Humar's smile faltered, his expression tightening like a wound closing under strain. Without a word, he turned and strode through the open door, his heavy boots thudding against the tilted floor, uneven from the crash. Noir followed, his eyes scanning the dim corridor where faint, dying lights cast erratic shadows on the walls. Twisted metal and shattered screens loomed like ghostly remnants of a forgotten past.

The filtered air reeked of burnt circuits and stale oxygen, a suffocating stench that clung to the back of Noir's throat like ash.

They entered a larger chamber—once a hub of bustling activity, now hollow and desolate. The floor sloped unnaturally, the entire structure listing as if the ship were caught in a slow, inevitable collapse. A distant creaking echoed through the stillness, like the pained groan of a wounded beast.

Saffron, her vibrant green skin a stark contrast to the dull grays of the ship's interior, grasped Noir's arm with all three of her right hands. Her breath came in quick, shallow bursts, her wide eyes darting nervously around the room. *I'm scared, Noir.*

Noir pulled her closer, his voice soft but steady, carrying a quiet confidence. *There's nothing to fear, Saffron. I'm here. I'll protect you.*

"I know," she whispered, her voice trembling like the fading hum of a tuning fork. "But I'm still scared."

Noir couldn't blame her. Something was deeply wrong here. It wasn't just the eerie silence or the oppressive atmosphere; it was a bone-deep unease that defied explanation. This was the kind of fear that no logic could dispel—a primal dread that whispered of things twisted and unnatural.

They moved cautiously across the slanted floor, their footsteps ringing out in the stillness, the rhythmic clink of metal underfoot the only sound. Ahead, a half-spherical door loomed ominously, a sickly yellow light spilling through a jagged crack at its center. Humar, his voice tinged with misplaced excitement, pointed toward it. "There they are! My crew's inside!"

Noir knocked on the door, the dull thud of metal echoing in the confined space. From within came a muffled, unintelligible response. He pushed the door open, revealing a chamber smaller than the last, its sloping floor uneven and precarious. The room was crammed against the engine bay, the air colder and carrying a faint metallic tang that clung to his senses.

Scattered around the room were people in tattered suits smeared with grease and grime, their stillness unsettling. They were slumped in awkward, unnatural positions, their eyes wide and vacant, staring at nothing.

Humar stepped inside, his bravado dimming as his gaze swept over his crew. Saffron let out a muffled scream, her six arms wrapping tightly around Noir in a desperate embrace. He could feel her trembling through their suits.

"What is it, Saffron?" Noir asked quietly, his voice steady despite the growing knot of unease tightening in his chest.

"I don't know what they are," Saffron whispered, her voice quaking with terror. "They're… wrong. I'm scared."

Humar strode to the center of the room, his arms spreading wide as if to greet an audience. *"My boys and girls! I've missed you! How have you been?"*

The crew remained unnervingly still, their unblinking eyes fixed in empty stares. Only those closest to Humar moved, raising their arms in slow, mechanical waves. Their jerky, disjointed movements resembled broken machinery struggling against rust.

Undeterred, Humar pressed on, his voice forced and cheerfully strained. *"I didn't expect you all to survive. It's a damn miracle! The gods of anarchy must want us to continue our adventure, eh?"*

Silence answered him, thick and oppressive, wrapping around the room like an unseen shroud. Noir watched as a Drikhm woman with horns, her gaunt figure swaying and her dull eyes unfocused, slowly rose from the back of the room. Her movements were labored, as though she were pushing against an invisible current. She approached Humar with heavy footsteps, her shadow stretching grotesquely in the sickly yellow light.

"Kehlani," Humar said, his voice faltering slightly. *"Feels like ages since I saw you last. But hey, no worries now. I'm here to take you back."*

When Kehlani spoke, her voice rasped and metallic, devoid of any warmth. "You'll take us?"

Noir flinched at the sound, a chill rippling through him. The voices of Humar's crew didn't align with their forms; they were hollow, more like something attempting to imitate human speech—an eerie echo of life.

Humar nodded eagerly, the cheer returning to his voice. "That's right. Your captain's back! We'll get the band together again! New adventures! We're going to plunder, loot, pillage! We'll kill! We'll take! We'll get new weapons, new technologies! I've been planning this ever since they thought they had me frozen in cryo sleep—"

"Will there be people?" interrupted Boxis, a burly Moughs with white fangs and pointed ears. His voice cracked, brimming with a manic intensity.

Humar blinked, momentarily thrown. "People? Of course there'll be people. We're not raiding empty space, are we?"

Boxis's laughter erupted suddenly—a grating, hollow cackle that sent a ripple of unease through the room. It spread quickly, infecting the rest of the crew. Their laughter wasn't joyous; it was unsettling, mirthless, bouncing off the walls in a dissonant chorus that made Noir's skin crawl.

As the laughter finally ebbed, Humar's cheerful facade began to crack. "How have you been surviving here?" he asked, his tone sharper.

A long pause followed, the crew exchanging blank looks. Finally, a red-skinned Ghraam woman with jagged bony protrusions, Cioni, replied in the same flat, monotonous tone. "That is unknown."

"Unknown?" Humar repeated, his voice rising with incredulity. *"What do you mean 'unknown'? I'm asking how you've managed all this time."*

Cioni fixed Humar with a cold, unblinking stare. *"There was an explosion. Everything became unknown."*

Humar's eyes darted around the room, his frustration mounting. "What do you mean everything became unknown?"

"Correct," came the flat response, echoed by the others as if rehearsed.

"Everything became unknown," they chanted in unison, the phrase morphing into a chilling mantra that filled the room, pressing in on Noir from all sides.

"Everything became unknown…." "Everything became unknown…."

"Enough!" Humar shouted, his voice slicing through the eerie refrain. His glare swept across the room, his anger palpable. *"You're lying! You all remember! You just don't want to tell me!"*

Noir's gaze hardened. There was something deeply wrong here, something off about the crew's behavior. It was as if their minds were stuck in a loop, severed from reality. He watched as Humar's face twisted with frustration, and a thought crept into his mind: why was Humar so desperate for answers? This wasn't just about survival. It was about something more.

Boxis rose slowly, his frame unfurling like a dying tree until he loomed over them, a towering shadow against the flickering yellow light spilling from the cracked door. Standing at least seven feet tall, perhaps more, his body was a grotesque patchwork of charred flesh and jagged scars. His right arm hung limp, swaying slightly with each shallow movement, though he made no sound of breath. His vacant eyes carried a dark, simmering resentment—not aimed at anyone in particular but seemingly directed at existence itself.

"We are lying to you?" Boxis's voice rumbled, like stone grinding against stone, devoid of emotion, as though spoken by someone who had long since discarded the memory of feeling.

Humar's face twisted, his cyborg eye flickering an ominous red. "Yes! You fuckers are lying to me!" Each word dripped with venom, his eyes wild and unhinged. His fingers twitched around the grip of his gun, the movement almost imperceptible but dangerous.

"Why?" Boxis asked, his tone flat, as though genuinely baffled by the accusation. His head tilted with the stiff, deliberate motion of a rusted automaton.

"Because you won't tell me where you hid the Osfronite orbs! You're trying to screw me over!" Humar's shout echoed through the chamber, the sound ricocheting off the dented walls like a trapped animal's desperate cry. The air thickened—not just with the stench of burning wires and chemical residue but with a suffocating tension, coiling tighter with every passing second.

Boxis's gaze shifted, drifting past Humar and over his shoulder. He stared vacantly into the distance, as though Humar's words were nothing but static, drowned out by the white noise of some internal void. He didn't flinch when Humar shoved him. The force sent Boxis sprawling to the floor with a dull, echoing thud, his massive body landing awkwardly like a toppled monument. He lay there, his limbs splayed at unnatural angles, unmoving. He didn't bother to rise. He didn't even seem to notice.

A laugh tore through the silence, sharp and shrill, void of joy. It started with Kehlani—a broken, jagged cackle clawing its way from her throat. Soon the others joined in, their voices merging into a discordant chorus of lifeless mirth. It was the laughter of madness, stripped of humanity, sanity, or warmth. Noir felt it seep into his bones, cold and corrosive, as if the sound itself had a physical weight, eroding him from the inside.

Humar's face reddened, his rage bubbling over like a boiling cauldron. He bared his teeth and stomped his boot into the floor, the metallic clang reverberating through the room. "Are you backstabbing bastards not going to tell me where you hid the Osfronites?" His voice cracked, thick with desperation, raw and ugly. He was a man teetering on the edge, and the ground beneath him was crumbling.

A Doctl man, gray-skinned and stooped, his six eyes glinting like pools of black oil, spoke up. His voice, more croak than coherent speech, rasped through the air. "Can't even remember if we're still alive or not, let alone some Osfronites."

Cioni, her crimson skin vivid even under the dull, artificial light, glanced at Humar with an unsettling detachment. Her expression carried a faint curiosity, as though she were studying an unusual specimen. "What exactly is this Osfronite you keep mentioning?"

Humar's finger tightened on the trigger, the barrel of his gun hovering inches from Cioni's forehead. His breathing was ragged, his mechanical eye flickering erratically, glowing with uneven pulses of crimson light. "Now you're telling me you don't even know what an Osfronite is?"

Cioni's unblinking gaze remained fixed on him, her face betraying nothing. "Maybe I do. Maybe I don't. It is not known. Truthfully, everything is unknown."

Humar's eyes burned with fury. "Do you remember me?"

Silence. Cioni stared through him, as if he were a shadow rather than flesh and blood.

Humar lowered the gun slightly, though his frustration boiled over into something darker, more volatile. His snarl twisted into a grimace, spittle flecking his lips as he shouted, "You think I came all the way here just to save your sorry asses?" His voice cracked, rising into a shrill, brittle pitch, the sound of a man fighting against his own unraveling sanity. He stamped his foot hard against the floor, the metallic clang reverberating in the stillness. "No! I didn't go through all that just to save you worthless scumbags! No one in their right mind steals an etherean-class spaceship and crosses this godforsaken region for fun! I came for my Osfronites! Where are my Osfronites? Tell me!"

For the briefest moment, Cioni's expression flickered—something almost like recognition flared and then faded in her vacant stare. She stammered, "W-wait… let me ask…"

Humar leaned closer, his face inches from hers, his breath hot and sharp as the barrel of his gun trembled in his hand. *"Who the fuck are you going to ask?"*

"The—there—ah—I mean—it's the—" Cioni stammered, her eyes darting frantically, confusion settling over her features like a dense fog.

Humar's face twisted further, a storm of rage and disbelief swirling in his expression. His voice dropped, low and dangerous, every word laced with venom. *"A cat in gloves catches no mice. I need to make an example, to remind all of you who I am."*

Noir's heart raced as he watched the exchange, terror creeping into his thoughts. What was the mad cyborg going to do now?

Humar spoke through clenched teeth, his words a chilling ultimatum. *"I will kill each of you, one by one, every ten seconds. The only way to stop me is to tell me where you've hidden my Osfronites."*

Humar aimed his gun at Cioni's head again, and Noir realized with chilling clarity that Humar truly intended to shoot her after ten seconds.

Noir stepped forward, the cold crawl of dread snaking up his spine. "Listen, Humar—"

Humar whipped around, his mechanical eye blazing. *"You shut up! I didn't come here to preach religion! If I don't kill one or two of them, they'll never learn—"*

Noir cut him off, his voice calm but firm, a razor slicing through the escalating chaos. "Who exactly do you want to kill?"

"This red Ghraam right here!" Humar snarled, jabbing the gun toward Cioni.

Noir's voice softened, its clarity sharp enough to pierce the mounting tension. *"What's the point of killing someone who's already dead?"*

Humar froze. His grip on the gun faltered, the resolve in his expression unraveling. He turned slowly, his wide eyes searching Noir's face for a trace of deceit. *"What did you just say?"*

Noir drew a steady breath, meeting Humar's frantic gaze. "They're already dead."

Humar's face blanched. "Dead? All of them?"

"Yes," Noir said, his voice steady, though the unease in his chest threatened to surface. He gestured to the crew, their unnaturally still bodies slumped in grotesque mockeries of life. *"There's no oxygen on this moon—just toxic gas. Your crew has no helmets. And they aren't breathing. Look for yourself."*

Humar's eyes darted between the motionless figures, panic and disbelief warring on his face. His hands trembled, the gun slipping slightly in his grasp. *"They aren't breathing?"*

"No," Noir said, his tone unyielding, though his own sense of dread churned beneath the surface.

"Then how the hell are they talking to me?" Humar's voice cracked, the question hanging in the air like a fragile thread about to snap.

Noir hesitated, his thoughts racing. "I don't know for sure, but I think—"

"You think what?" Humar's voice was raw, his bravado dissolving into desperation.

Noir's gaze swept the room, his voice dropping to a near whisper. "I think something is controlling the corpses of your crew—like puppets."

Humar's face twisted into a grimace of disbelief. A hollow, desperate laugh bubbled up from his lips, the sound jagged and broken.

"Stop fucking around, man. It's not funny." But the laugh was hollow, the sound of a man teetering on the edge of a crumbling cliff, staring into an unfathomable abyss.

Around them, the crew's eyes blinked in unison, the synchronized motion sending a sharp shiver down Noir's spine. The temperature in the room seemed to drop, the air growing heavier, laced with an intangible chill. Noir's tongue tingled with the metallic taste of fear as he watched the crew. And then he felt it—a presence, old and patient, lurking unseen in the shadows. It was watching them. It didn't care about the living. It never had.

Noir's breath hitched as the realization struck: Humar didn't believe him, and the cyborg's mania was teetering on the edge of violence. Humar's finger twitched on the trigger, his eyes wild and unfocused, flickering erratically between fury and fear. Noir's gaze swept the room, cataloging every movement. Kehlani had shifted subtly—almost imperceptibly—from her spot. She now stood by the door, the only exit from this cursed chamber. Noir's pulse quickened. If she sealed the door, there would be no escape.

Boxis was no longer sprawled on the floor like a discarded puppet. Somehow, he had repositioned himself, now standing to their flank, towering and grotesque. The rest of Humar's crew—Cioni, the old Doctl man, and others— were closing in, their movements slow but deliberate, encircling them like a pack of predators. Their eyes, lifeless and glassy like marbles, fixed unwaveringly on Noir and Humar. A shiver ran down Noir's spine. It was unnatural to see dead people move. There was no mistaking it now— these weren't just corpses. They were something far worse.

Noir took a cautious step back, aligning himself beside Saffron. He leaned in close, his voice a faint whisper in her helmet, barely audible. "Saffron."

"What is it?" Her voice trembled, taut with fear, the tension in the air gnawing at her composure.

"Wrap your arms around me. Hold on as tightly as you can."

"Why?" Her wide eyes darted between Noir and the encroaching crew, her confusion mounting.

"I can't explain right now. Just do it. Be ready."

"Ready for what?"

"I don't know yet." Noir's clipped response betrayed his focus, his attention shifting back to the advancing crew. He primed his weapon with deliberate precision, every movement slow and calculated. His gaze flicked to Humar, who, for the first time since Noir had met him, looked genuinely afraid. The towering cyborg's bravado had crumbled, his usual confidence replaced by raw panic.

"Everyone freeze! Don't fucking move an inch!" Humar's voice was shrill, cracking like brittle glass, but his command fell into a void of silence. The crew didn't stop. Another step forward, their movements eerily synchronized, their unblinking, glassy eyes locked on their former leader.

Humar's scream ripped through the air, feral and guttural, wrenched from the depths of his dread. He squeezed the trigger. The gun erupted with a deafening roar, a thunderous torrent of rapid gunfire that ricocheted through the chamber like rolling thunder. The muzzle flashed in staccato bursts, spitting a storm of bullets into the advancing crew. Sparks danced across the metal walls as bullets ricocheted, a high-pitched whine filling the space—a shriek of overstressed metal and raw kinetic energy.

But the crew didn't flinch.

Bullets tore into them, shredding flesh and fabric alike, but they kept moving, unphased and unfeeling. Cioni let out a guttural, broken laugh, her face splitting into a grotesque grin despite the gaping wounds that riddled her torso. Her laughter echoed through the chamber, bouncing off the walls—a sound so jarring, so deeply wrong, that it sent an icy shiver down Noir's spine.

Humar's expression twisted into raw, unfiltered horror. He turned to Noir, his eyes wide and glistening with a terror that clung to him like a second skin. Noir held his gaze for a moment, the fear reflected back at him like a fractured mirror, before Humar whipped around and fired another volley into his undying crew.

Noir could only watch, frozen, as the bullets tore into the advancing figures. But there was no blood, no spray of gore. Instead, black sludge oozed from the bullet wounds, squirming like living tentacles before retreating back into the bodies, sealing the injuries shut with a sick, fluid motion. The air vibrated with a low, menacing hiss—an animalistic sound that slithered beneath the discord of gunfire, like the breath of something ancient and malign stirring just beyond the veil of reality.

Saffron's scream pierced through the chaos, sharp and panicked. Her six arms wrapped tightly around Noir, trembling with fear. He could feel her pulse pounding against him, a frantic rhythm that mirrored his own. Noir grasped one of her arms, his fingers pressing firm and reassuring despite the tremor in his own hands. "Hold onto me. Do not let go, no matter what!" His voice was steady but urgent.

His other hand tightened around the grip of his gun. With a deft flick of his thumb, he activated its atomic blaster mode—a last-ditch gamble, reckless but necessary. Noir raised the weapon, not aiming at the abominations closing in around them but at the ceiling above. Heat surged through the gun, the barrel humming with barely contained starfire, ready to erupt. Noir steadied his aim, took a deep breath, and pulled the trigger.

The gun roared to life, unleashing a beam of searing white light that carved through the ceiling with brutal force. It wasn't a clean, controlled shot—this was raw, unrefined energy, a superheated plasma blast that erupted in a blinding explosion. The chamber rocked violently as the detonation tore through the air, the sound an ear-splitting crescendo that left Noir's ears ringing. Chunks of debris rained down, molten slag hissing and spitting as it struck the cold floor. The shockwave hit them like a physical force, reverberating through their bones.

Noir blinked against the blinding light, his vision swimming from the intensity of the flash. As the haze cleared, he saw the jagged hole he had carved into the ceiling—a gaping wound that exposed the sky above. The harsh, oppressive glow of the dwarf sun filtered in, casting elongated shadows through the swirling dust. The air was thick with the acrid stench of scorched metal and ozone, the sharp tang clawing at the back of Noir's throat, mixing with the bitter taste of sweat and fear.

The chamber trembled, groaning under the strain of the blast's aftermath. The residual heat from the atomic discharge clung to the air, pressing against their suits with an oppressive intensity. Noir's skin prickled, a sensation akin to a sunburn creeping just beneath the surface, while the deafening hum of energy reverberated through the chamber, rattling his teeth and shaking deep in his chest.

Above, the jagged maw in the ceiling framed a sky that was as hostile as the landscape below. Sickly green and yellow clouds churned in roiling chaos, resembling a festering wound torn open in the atmosphere. For a fleeting moment, Noir thought he saw movement—something vast and shadowy stirring within the toxic clouds—but when he blinked, it was gone. Around them, Humar's dead crew advanced with relentless determination, their lifeless eyes reflecting the dim, fractured light of a world devoid of meaning. The grotesque synchronization of their steps, their stiff, unnatural movements, sent shivers down Noir's spine. Against him, Saffron trembled violently, her grip tightening around his arm as though clinging to him was the only thing keeping her tethered to sanity.

Humar stood a short distance away, still firing, still screaming defiance into the void, but the futility of his actions was apparent. His bullets tore through the reanimated crew, but they didn't stop, didn't falter. It was as if the very laws of life and death had no place in this cursed chamber. Noir's mind raced with questions, unrelenting and unanswered: What were these creatures that controlled the dead? How had they evolved here, on this moon where survival itself defied all logic?

But there was no time for questions, no time to dwell on the horrors unraveling before him. Noir clenched his jaw, forcing himself to focus. His fingers moved with precise intent, securing his weapon magnetically to his right thigh. His free hand, still gripping Saffron tightly, found the ignition switch on his backpack. Without hesitation, he pressed it. A faint metallic click was followed by a low rumble as the lift engine sputtered to life, its vibrations traveling through his suit and into his very bones.

The engine's growl deepened into a throaty buzz, a sound that seemed almost too small for the monumental task ahead. Designed for single-person navigation, the engine now faced the grueling challenge of carrying two. Noir knew the strain would be immense— fuel efficiency would be pushed to its limits, and their speed would suffer—but there was no alternative. Survival demanded risks, and luxuries like speed and caution were sacrifices they couldn't afford to lament.

The rising hum of the engine drew the attention of Humar's dead crew. As one, their heads snapped toward the sound with unnatural precision, their glassy, lifeless eyes locking onto Noir and Saffron like predators scenting prey. Their movements were sudden, jerking into action with a terrifying urgency. Limbs flailed as they lunged toward the pair, their grotesque forms surging forward in a synchronized wave of death.

Noir's mind raced. There was no time to hesitate. He tapped into his ferrionics, the familiar surge of energy flooding through his legs, every muscle and tendon thrumming with amplified power. With a forceful kick, he launched off the ground, the impact sending a sharp jolt up his spine. The lift engine roared to life, flaring to full power, its jets igniting in a violent burst. The sudden propulsion catapulted them skyward, tearing through the air with a heatsoaked shimmer. Below, clawing hands reached for them, missing by mere inches as they shot through the gaping hole in the ceiling. Noir caught a fleeting glimpse of the chaos left behind—limbs flailing, bodies colliding in a frenzied scuffle—as the chamber and its horrifying occupants shrank into an unrecognizable blur.

The world spun and tumbled around them as Noir adjusted their trajectory, steering them toward the heavens. The wind howled past, sharp and biting, stinging his exposed skin where the seal on his helmet had slightly shifted during the rush. The air was thick with a metallic tang, each breath feeling like needles scraping down his throat. The swirling green fog and phosphorescent dust clung to the atmosphere, casting an eerie, otherworldly glow that danced in jagged patterns across the barren wasteland below. A faint electric charge prickled along the surface of his suit, making his hair stand on end—a sensation like the static buildup before a violent storm.

He held Saffron tightly, her six arms wrapped around him in a desperate grip. Her body trembled against his, her fear palpable even through the layers of protective gear. Noir could feel the rapid cadence of her breathing—sharp, irregular gasps punctuated by occasional shudders as she fought to suppress her rising panic.

"Don't let go of me, Saffron," Noir commanded, his voice calm but edged with urgency. The words were transmitted directly into her helmet through the comm system, crackling slightly with static.

Her response came as a whisper, barely audible over the rush of wind and the persistent hum of the lift engine. "I still can't believe we made it out alive."

Noir kept his gaze fixed on the hazy horizon, scanning for any sign of the scout ship. His tone remained firm, steady. "Don't be so sure just yet, Saffron."

"What do you mean?" she asked, her voice tight with anxiety. She looked up at him, her wide eyes reflecting the ghostly glow of the swirling fog around them.

Noir's jaw tightened, his instincts screaming warnings he couldn't yet articulate. "It's not over. Not until we're back on the ship. Stay focused."

"I doubt those things will let us go so easily," Noir said grimly, his mind haunted by the unsettling intelligence he had seen flicker in those lifeless eyes.

"Why? Why do you say that, Noir?" Saffron's voice was thick with dread, her grip on him tightening almost to the point of pain.

Noir hesitated, his gaze fixed on the shifting fog around them, then spoke with quiet certainty. "Those creatures, they've only played with corpses before. But now they've encountered something alive. From what I've seen, they're not mindless husks. They're curious. They're cunning. And that makes them infinitely more dangerous."

"Oh my god!" Saffron gasped, her voice breaking into a half-sob. She had wished for happy, playful animals— something innocent and endearing. Instead, she'd stumbled into a waking nightmare.

"Yes," Noir said sharply, his tone edged with warning. "Stay on alert. And don't lose your gun."

Saffron's voice wavered, a mix of fear and frustration. "I told you, Noir, I don't know how to shoot a gun. I've never done it before—"

"It doesn't matter," Noir cut her off, his eyes darting through the swirling green clouds. "When the time comes, you'll know what to do."

"How?" she asked, her tone small and vulnerable, like a child lost in the middle of a storm. "How will I know?"

"Your survival instinct will take over," Noir said, his words weighted with a resigned wisdom. "It's what makes us 'human-like.' It doesn't matter where we come from or what we look like. Across the universe, we're all driven by the same primal need to survive."

They ascended higher, hundreds of meters above the jagged terrain below. The desolate landscape stretched out beneath them, a haunting expanse of twisted rock formations and shifting, ash-like dust. Above, the sky was an unrelenting chaos—a churning sea of green fog streaked with flashes of lightning. The bolts ripped through the dense clouds, illuminating the toxic atmosphere with blinding light. Each flash left afterimages seared into Noir's vision, and every strike brought a deafening crack, a sound like fabric being torn apart by immense, invisible hands. The air vibrated with the force of each lightning strike, a low, resonating hum that Noir felt deep in his bones.

As they climbed higher, Noir became acutely aware of Saffron's trembling. She clung to him as though he were the last stable thing in a collapsing world. Her quivering wasn't just from the cold; it was the raw, unfiltered expression of a terror that had burrowed deep into her psyche. He could feel her trust in him, the way she relied on him to keep her tethered to life amid the chaos. That unspoken dependence spurred a fierce determination in Noir. He would see this through. He would get them both out of this nightmare, no matter the cost.

Through the murky haze, the silhouette of the scout ship emerged, a dormant giant looming in the distance like a prehistoric beast. Half-buried and inert, its massive form was indistinct but undeniably familiar. Even under the dim, erratic light, its harsh, utilitarian contours stood in stark contrast to the surreal and almost alien environment surrounding it. This was no ordinary wreck—it was a relic from another time, another place. And for Noir, it was a symbol of hope, a chance at safety in an unforgiving world.

The soft ping of Noir's suit sensors broke through his thoughts, signaling that they were now within range. With a single mental command, he activated the ship's systems. A distant rumble vibrated through the air as the dormant vessel flickered to life, its engines stirring after years of silence. Relief washed over Noir like a fleeting tide, easing the tension that had clung to him since the moment he crossed paths with Humar.

"We've arrived, Saffron," Noir said, his voice a weary mix of exhaustion and quiet triumph. "Prepare to land."

"I'm ready," she replied, though the tremor in her voice betrayed the lingering aftershocks of their ordeal.

The lift mechanism responded to Noir's slightest thought, as if an extension of his own will. The spacesuit's visor didn't literally read his mind, but it might as well have. The compact onboard AI—no larger than a thumb—was engineered to sense the faintest muscle twitches and the most subtle shifts in his body. Every movement was analyzed, calculated, and executed in an instant. It wasn't dependent on the hypermind's vast processing power, but it didn't need to be. This technology was a marvel of engineering, a seamless blend of man and machine that made flight feel second nature, almost instinctive.

Noir could steer, pivot, and adjust with mere thoughts, his body and the suit operating as one. The suit's surface was sleek and unencumbered—no buttons, no controls to distract or slow him down. It was a symbiotic connection, fine-tuned to perfection, allowing Noir to navigate the hostile atmosphere with unmatched precision. Even so, certain functions, such as activating or shutting down the lift engine, still required manual input.

As Noir carefully adjusted the power output, the suit responded with flawless grace. He came to a near stop, descending with a fluidity that defied the volatile environment around him. The landing was soft, the suit expertly absorbing the impact and dispersing the force across his body. Saffron remained securely held in his grasp, her weight barely noticeable against the suit's adaptive systems.

The ground beneath them shifted and heaved, a surreal expanse of bubbling ponds and steaming rocks. The air was thick with the acrid tang of sulfur, each breath oppressive despite the suit's advanced filtration systems. Heat radiated from the volatile terrain, seeping through the suit's insulation in a relentless assault. Noir's helmet worked overtime to filter the toxic atmosphere, yet a faint bitterness still lingered on the back of his tongue, a grim reminder of the planet's hostility. Steam hissed intermittently from the surrounding rocks, sending scalding vapor into the air. The droplets clung to his visor, warping the already dismal view into a kaleidoscope of distorted shapes.

Saffron clung to him, her six arms wrapped around him with a vice-like grip. Through the comms, Noir could hear her labored breaths, each one shaky and uneven. She trembled violently against him, and Noir didn't need to guess—if she let go, her legs would give out entirely. With a firm yet fluid motion, Noir adjusted her position. Sliding one arm under her knees and the other around her waist, he lifted her effortlessly. Her slight frame, even with the added bulk of her suit, was negligible in his grasp.

Saffron gasped, the sound sharp and startled, her breath hitching as she found herself cradled securely against his chest. Her visor fogged slightly with rapid exhalations, soft clouds obscuring her view of the treacherous terrain. Noir's strength, the solid steadiness of his arms, and the faint warmth emanating from his suit provided an anchor amidst the chaos. She clung to him tighter, her heart pounding in a tangled mix of lingering fear and an unexpected sense of safety.

Noir's boots thudded heavily against the scout ship's steps, each impact reverberating through the metallic surface. The combined weight of his suit and Saffron pressed into the reinforced metal, a testament to the strain of their trek across the hostile environment. At last, the ship's door slid open with a smooth mechanical whine, its sound cutting sharply through the ambient chaos outside.

Once inside, the door sealed shut behind them with a definitive hiss, locking out the oppressive heat and cacophony of the world beyond. The silence hit like a physical force, an unwelcome pressure that rang in Noir's ears and made the stillness inside the ship feel almost alien. For a moment, he stood motionless, adjusting to the sudden absence of the planet's relentless hostility.

They stood in the quarantine chamber, a sterile and clinical space engineered to purge every trace of organic or inorganic contaminants from their suits. The walls, sleek and reflective, were lined with rows of nozzles and vents that hissed to life, spraying them with precise sequences of chemical solutions. The sharp, antiseptic scent filled the air, tinged with the metallic tang of ozone from sterilizing rays. Overhead, powerful UV lights blazed, casting harsh violet shadows that danced along the walls, amplifying the room's already claustrophobic atmosphere.

The system cycled through its cleaning protocols, scouring every surface of their suits with ruthless efficiency. Every molecule of alien matter was obliterated, leaving no margin for error. Air was sucked from the chamber with a deafening rush, creating a brief but uncomfortable vacuum that pressed against their bodies. Noir's suit compensated automatically, adjusting internal pressure to stabilize him, though the sensation was no less unsettling.

Noir stood motionless, his posture rigid as the process stretched on. He resisted the urge to fidget or pace— actions that would betray the tension simmering beneath his calm exterior. Every second in this chamber felt intolerable, a reminder of how desperately they needed to leave this moon. But the quarantine procedure was non-negotiable; the scout ship's systems wouldn't permit entry without full clearance, and any risk of bringing unknown contaminants aboard the mothership, Wayfarer, was unthinkable.

His expression remained composed, his features schooled into a mask of control. A captain couldn't afford to show impatience or fear, not when the survival of others depended on his steadiness. Yet, beneath the calm facade, Noir's mind churned with urgency, each moment stretching endlessly as the system's relentless precision dragged on.

Finally, after what felt like an eternity, the chamber's green light flickered on. A soft chime signaled the end of the procedure, and the sealed door slid open with a sharp hiss. Noir stepped through, carrying Saffron into the main chamber of the ship.

The transition was almost jarring—moving from the sterile, blinding light of the quarantine chamber to the ship's subdued, familiar interior. The hum of the ship's life support systems wrapped around them like a comforting blanket, its rhythmic pulse grounding them in the normalcy of their vessel. It wasn't safety, not yet, but it was a step closer.

Noir gently lowered Saffron onto one of the crew chairs, its cushioned surface instantly conforming to her form with the precision of Etherean engineering. The spacesuits provided by the Etherean shipbuilders were marvels of technological innovation, designed to adapt seamlessly to the wearer's body. Their inner linings maintained even pressure, offering both protection and comfort. But even with all their advancements, the suits could feel oppressive after prolonged use. Noir could see the toll in Saffron's expression—the faint glassiness in her wide eyes, the weariness etched into every line of her face. Fear lingered there, like an unshakable shadow.

Working methodically, Noir unzipped her suit, careful not to jostle her unnecessarily. The suit parted with a soft hiss, releasing a faint puff of pressurized air that dissipated quickly in the cabin. As the restrictive material peeled away, Noir noticed how pale Saffron's skin had become, slick with sweat. She shivered slightly as the cooler air inside the ship brushed against her exposed arms, the chill contrasting sharply with the heat that had been trapped within the suit.

Noir's hands moved with practiced precision, each action deliberate and measured to ensure her comfort. Once he had freed her from the suit, he leaned over the chair and unlocked the mechanism, allowing it to recline smoothly. With a soft click, the chair transformed into a makeshift bed, the cushioned surface flattening into something far more accommodating. Saffron sank into it, her body melting into the supportive material as the tension slowly began to drain from her frame.

For a moment, Noir simply stood there, watching her. The sharp lines of worry etched into his own face softened slightly as he saw the faintest hint of relief on hers. They had been through so much—chased by horrors, teetering on the brink of destruction—but at least, for now, they were safe. The nightmare was beginning to fade, though its echoes lingered in the corners of their minds.

Saffron's voice barely rose above a whisper, fragile and trembling in the quiet hum of the scout ship. *"Did we survive? Did we really survive, Noir?"*

Noir's hand stilled on the armrest, his gaze shifting from the flickering control panels to her face. Her words felt as delicate as mist, dissipating into the tension that still gripped the air. "It seems so," he replied, his tone low and uncertain. *"For now, it looks like we're out of danger."* But the tight coil of dread in his chest remained, unshaken by the brief reprieve. Even though the Wayfarer wasn't far off, the weight of what they'd just endured pressed heavily on him, refusing to fade.

He moved silently, his fingers finding the chair's recline controls. With a soft mechanical hum, the chair flattened into a bed, its joints clicking softly in the sterile quiet of the cabin. Saffron exhaled a deep sigh of relief as she sank into it, the crinkling fabric beneath her offering the first semblance of comfort in what felt like an eternity. The sharp metallic tang of the ship's interior lingered in the air, mingling with the faint ozone from the air recyclers. It was a cold, clinical scent, impersonal and devoid of warmth, doing little to calm their frayed nerves.

Noir adjusted the mechanism with slow, deliberate precision, his focus on the task as if trying to steady his own thoughts. But when he straightened, his breath hitched. Saffron's face was closer than he had anticipated, her presence suddenly and sharply real. He hadn't noticed before how her fatigue softened her features, how it made her seem more human, more vulnerable. Her deep brown eyes held a tired warmth, steady yet weighted by everything they had endured. They seemed to pull him in, locking him in place.

Strands of her rich, dark hair framed her face, catching the soft glow of the overhead lights. The subtle shadows played across her skin, highlighting the gentle curves of her cheekbones, the faint lines of exhaustion that only deepened her natural beauty.

Her gaze didn't waver. Noir's heart stuttered, the steady rhythm faltering for a moment. He couldn't move, couldn't find the words he knew he should say. His mind, usually sharp and precise, felt hazy, clouded like the drift of stars across a nebula. For a brief moment, the universe seemed to still, and all that existed was the space between them.

Saffron's hand lifted slowly, her fingers brushing the edge of his jaw. The touch was light yet electrifying, like the faint hum of a charged particle in the still vacuum of space. Her skin was warm against the coolness of his, a sensation both grounding and surreal.

"Noir," she whispered, her voice fragile, raw.

His throat tightened, and he managed to reply, though his voice was quieter than he intended. "Yes?" His gaze locked onto hers, drawn to the vulnerability that seemed to stretch infinitely in her eyes.

"Thank you for saving my life," she said, her fingers lingering on his skin, her words trembling with sincerity. "Thank you so much."

He tried to smile, but the expression was fleeting, uncertain. "Well," he began, his voice cracking slightly, *"I saved both of us. A solo adventure didn't seem all that appealing."*

Her lips quirked in a faint attempt at humor, but the expression didn't reach her eyes. "You could've escaped on your own. You didn't have to come back for me." There was disbelief in her tone, a quiet astonishment, as though the concept of someone risking themselves for another was foreign, alien.

Noir blinked, his brow furrowing as confusion settled in. "Why would I leave you behind? That's not—"

Saffron's thumb moved over his lips in a gentle, intimate gesture, silencing him. The touch lingered for a fraction of a second before she released him, leaning back as her hand fell to her side. "That's how you survive in space," she said, her tone matter-of-fact but laced with an undertone of sadness that hung in the air. "Everyone fends for themselves. That's what I was taught."

Noir's expression darkened at her words, a flicker of something deeper crossing his face—anger, not at her, but at the life that had shaped this belief. He could see it now, the hardened edges in her demeanor, the quiet resignation in her tone. Saffron hadn't just been taught survival in space; she'd been taught that trust was a weakness, that loyalty was a luxury afforded only to fools.

"I don't believe that," Noir said, his voice steady, firm. "That's not what I was taught."

Her smile returned, softer this time, more genuine, though tinged with a trace of vulnerability. *"Yes, I've noticed that you're… different."* She paused, her eyes narrowing slightly as though she were studying him more deeply, as though some truth had only just now dawned on her. And then it struck her, the realization settling in like a quiet revelation.

He wasn't enhanced. No genetic modifications, no artificial augmentations. Noir was just a man—a human in the most ordinary sense, navigating an extraordinary and unforgiving universe.

Having sensed her realization, something inside Noir shifted. He stood up, retreating to the pilot's seat, his movements deliberate yet heavy with unspoken weight. Settling into the chair, his hands began to glide over the controls with mechanical precision, each press of a button grounding him. The cool texture of the dashboard beneath his fingertips was a stark contrast to the unease swirling within him. He felt exposed, vulnerable in a way he hadn't anticipated.

Behind him, Saffron's voice broke through his thoughts, soft but clear. "Do you know the best thing that happened?"

Noir chuckled, though the sound rang hollow, devoid of warmth. "We got rid of Humar Danjon," he said, shaking his head. "And his crew, for that matter."

Saffron let out a light laugh, a sound like birdsong against the sterile hum of the ship. "Yes. I don't know if there was any other way we could've gotten rid of him."

"No," Noir agreed, his tone grim, his gaze fixed on the control panel. "Sometimes it takes one evil to destroy another."

Her laughter faded, replaced by a quieter, more contemplative tone. "You're not evil, Noir. You're the best person I've ever met. Does that mean you couldn't have done anything against Humar?"

Noir glanced over his shoulder, a faint shadow of a smile touching his lips. "You don't know me, Saffron. You've only known me a few days."

"And that was enough," she replied, her gaze steady, her voice tinged with a conviction that caught him off guard. *"You're not like other men. There's something in you… something special."*

For a moment, Noir didn't respond. Her words hung in the air, filling the quiet space between them. He wondered what she thought she'd seen in him—what part of him she found worthy of admiration. The silence stretched, yet it didn't feel uncomfortable.

The control panel blinked to life with a steady green light, pulling Noir's attention back to the task at hand. His fingers hovered over the ignition switch as the diagnostics finished their final checks. With a firm press, he initiated the fuel flow to the dual plasma engines. A deep, resonant hum vibrated through the ship's hull, signaling their readiness to leave this cursed moon behind—forever, or so he hoped.

"What do you think happened to Humar Danjon?" Saffron's voice broke the silence again, softer this time but laced with an edge of unease.

Noir shook his head, his eyes never leaving the display. "It's hard to say. He's… strange. More machine than man now, but not in a way that makes him better." His voice darkened, each word steeped in bitter truth. "Humar Danjon isn't just another bad guy. He's probably the worst human in recent history. A man who carved a cyber-mind into his skull, blending flesh with machinery until you couldn't tell where one ended and the other began."

Saffron gasped, her voice edged with unfiltered fear. "How terrifying!"

Noir tried to dismiss it with a shrug, but the stiffness in his movements betrayed him as he checked the last of the flight systems. "We got rid of him. There's no need to worry anymore. That pain in the ass won't be a problem." He hesitated briefly, then added, "Saffron, I'm starting the engines now. Secure yourself."

Saffron sat upright, reaching for the safety belt. But as her gaze drifted toward the transparent viewport, her body locked in place. Her face turned ghostly pale.

"Noir!"

Her scream tore through the cabin, ricocheting off the cold, metallic walls. It wasn't the cry of someone startled—it was guttural, primal, the sound of a soul staring into the abyss. Noir snapped around in his seat, his heart thundering as he followed her line of sight.

Standing just beyond the viewport was Humar Danjon.

Noir's blood froze. Time seemed to stretch endlessly in that moment. Humar's figure loomed in the faint, eerie glow of the moon's surface. His body was twisted unnaturally, his face a grotesque contortion, as if struggling against some force that defied comprehension. Yet, that wasn't what sent a chill down Noir's spine.

Coiling around Humar's body were writhing, sinewy tendrils— vines that resembled living nightmares more than plant life. They glistened under the moon's spectral light, pulsating with a sinister, alien energy, as though forged from living shadow. The tendrils dragged at Humar, their slick surfaces gleaming with an unidentifiable substance. He fought against them, his limbs thrashing wildly, alloyfused hands straining to break free, but it was a losing battle. The cosmic entity—whatever it was—had him firmly in its grasp.

"Noir! Start the engines! NOW!" Saffron's voice pierced the air, each word rising in pitch, raw and trembling with terror.

Noir's hand shot to the engine controls, his mind spiraling into overdrive. The ship's shield was active; he was certain of that. Humar couldn't breach it, not even with the advanced weapons embedded in his body. The shields would hold. They had to. They could escape.

And yet...

Noir froze.

Humar's face was contorted in sheer panic. His eyes—those cold, machine-enhanced eyes—were wide, desperate, brimming with an emotion Noir had never seen in him before: raw, unrestrained terror. Humar was screaming, but no sound pierced the silence within the ship's shielded confines. His mechanical limbs unleashed bursts of energy, futile blasts that only caused the tendrils to constrict further, dragging him inch by inch toward the dark, yawning crevice of the moon where they had originated.

"Noir, please! START THE ENGINES!" Saffron's voice cracked, her words trembling as she tugged frantically at her safety belt. Her eyes darted wildly between Noir and the viewport, desperation etched into her every feature. "He's going to break through, Noir! We'll all die if you don't—"

Noir's hand hovered over the engine switch. His heart hammered against his ribcage, each beat a deafening reminder of the choice he faced. But something deep within him—something instinctual, primal, buried in the recesses of his conscience—held him back.

Humar Danjon was a monster. A man who had willingly chosen to abandon his humanity, becoming more machine than flesh—a construct of cold logic and cruelty. Yet now, that monster was terrified. Begging. Pleading for his life.

Noir swallowed hard, his throat as parched as the barren moonscapes he had once explored. Could he let a man, no matter how despicable, be consumed by some cosmic nightmare and still call himself human? Could he stand by and witness another living being devoured by something so unnatural, so unspeakably horrifying, and emerge unchanged?

His hand slipped away from the engine switch.

"What are you doing?!" Saffron's voice cracked, each word trembling with panic, nearly incoherent. *"Noir, start the engines! What the hell are you doing?!"*

"I… I have to help him," Noir murmured, his voice distant and uncertain, as though he couldn't quite grasp his own words.

Saffron gawked at him, her face a battle between horror and disbelief. "What did you just say?!"

"I have to help Humar," Noir repeated, his voice stronger now, steadier. "He's a human being. I can't—"

"HE'S NOT HUMAN!" Saffron screamed, her voice ripping through the cabin like a shockwave. "He's worse than that thing out there! He'll kill us the second you let him in! You KNOW that!"

"I know." Noir's voice was eerily calm now, his tone resigned. "But I can't leave him behind."

Saffron's eyes darted around wildly, her chest heaving as she gasped for air. "Why are you saying this? What kind of man are you?!"

Noir rose to his feet, his movements slow, deliberate, as if the weight of his decision pressed on his every joint. He turned to her, his gaze shadowed by an emotion she couldn't quite identify. "You said earlier that I was different," he said quietly. "Maybe you were right. I'm not like the others." He paused, his voice tinged with bitterness. "I think I'm a fool."

Without another word, Noir stepped toward the airlock. His hand trembled as he reached for the control panel, and the hiss of the mechanism pierced the tense silence of the cabin. The door slid open, and the cool, alien air of the moon swept in, laced with the faint, indescribable scent of something ancient—something timeless.

For a brief moment, Noir felt a flicker of resentment—directed inward, toward himself. Then outward, toward his mother, the woman who had instilled in him a conscience that felt like a curse in a place like this. Why did she have to make him this way? Why couldn't he be like the others—cold, calculating, willing to do whatever was necessary?

CHAPTER 7

THE FREEDOM SURGERY

The dual plasma engines hummed beneath the metallic shell of the scout ship—a deep, steady rumble that spoke of the raw power coursing through the vessel. Outside, the swirling storms of the gas giant X-E9013 framed the infinite black void of space. They had just completed their final orbit of the barren moon and were now hurtling back toward the Wayfarer, their mothership, the only sanctuary in this desolate stretch of the universe.

Noir leaned over the console, his fingers moving deftly across the interface. The scout ship's communication module flickered to life, transmitting encrypted signals to the Wayfarer. The automatic feedback process began, and as soon as the confirmation flashed green, he exhaled, allowing himself a brief reprieve. He sank back into the chair, letting his eyes close for just a moment.

Then, something cold pressed against his neck. The unmistakable chill of metal.

Noir didn't need to open his eyes to know what it was.

The muzzle of a projectile gun—and there was only one person on this scout ship who would have it. Humar Danjon.

A slow, humorless chuckle sounded from behind him, each syllable steeped in venom. "What a moron," Humar spat, his voice like the rasp of corroded machinery grinding itself to pieces. *"Opening the scout ship's doors and letting me in. How stupid can one man be?"*

Noir had anticipated this. Humar's fury was palpable, radiating off him like heat waves, suffocating in the confines of the small cabin. Yet, even with cold steel pressed against his throat, Noir's heartbeat remained steady. He wouldn't give Humar the satisfaction of seeing fear.

"Look at you." Humar dug the muzzle of the gun harder against Noir's neck, his breath quick and jagged, each word dripping with raw, unrestrained rage. *"Letting me in just proves what an idiot you are."*

Noir could feel the heat of Humar's anger, almost tangible, searing against his skin like a burning aura. Still, he remained silent. His lack of reaction only fueled Humar's rage, a volatile storm ready to detonate at any second.

"You have no idea how much I want to empty this clip into your head," Humar hissed. His voice was jagged, each word sharp and unyielding. *"But I won't. You know why?"*

Noir remained calm. "No. Why?"

"Because," Humar leaned closer, his breath hot and rancid, "if I blow your brains out, I'll have to clean your blood and brain matter off this console. And I hate cleaning."

A wry smile tugged at Noir's lips. "Is that so?"

"I can't stand men like you," Humar continued, venom dripping from his words. "Naïve idiots with their noble ideas."

Noir's hand darted out in a flash, slapping the gun aside with a fluid, practiced motion. The cold metal left his skin, but Humar didn't fire. Noir knew he wouldn't.

"Humar," Noir said evenly, his voice steady, *I think you know exactly why you can't stand me. And it's not because I'm an idiot."*

Humar's lips curled into a sneer. "Oh? Enlighten me."

Noir turned in his chair, meeting Humar's dark, mechanical gaze without flinching. Behind those cold, augmented eyes, the faintest flicker of something human remained, buried beneath layers of machinery and unrelenting hatred. *"You can't stand me," Noir said slowly, "because I spared your life. And you can't figure out why."*

Humar's expression hardened, his jaw tightening like the gears of his cybernetic enhancements. *"I know why, you sanctimonious bastard!"*

"No," Noir said softly, his voice unnervingly calm, "you don't. You lack the capacity to understand something like that, Humar. But, for your peace of mind, I'll explain."

Humar's loathing radiated off him, almost tangible, twisting his face into a mask of pure contempt as he stared at Noir like he was the embodiment of every injustice in the universe. How humiliating it must have been—to be one of the galaxy's most feared beings, a cybernetic terror, and yet find himself saved by someone so ordinary, so infuriatingly human.

Noir's tone remained steady, almost disarmingly soothing in its reasoned clarity. *"The creatures on that moon,"* he began, "the cosmic animals—they're more intelligent than we've ever given them credit for. They extracted information from the minds of the dead, repurposed their knowledge, and used them like puppets. They're learning from us. Evolving."

"What the hell are you talking about?" Humar snarled, his anger flaring, sharp and volatile. *"What does that have to do with anything?"*

"If we leave behind the impression that a human will abandon another human in their time of need," Noir said quietly, his voice steady, "what message does that send to them?"

Humar's face contorted, first with confusion, then with rage. His mouth opened as if to respond, but for a moment, no words came. The silence stretched, heavy and suffocating, the weight of Noir's statement pressing down on them both.

And then Humar exploded.

"You son of a—!" His voice was raw, a feral roar ripping through the cabin. *"I'll kill you! I'll kill you, Noir! I'll end you once and for all!"*

Noir turned back to the control panel, seemingly unbothered by the outburst. His movements were calm, deliberate. "I don't care, Humar," he replied serenely, his tone unwavering. *"You can't threaten a man with death when he's already accepted it."*

Behind him, Humar seethed. His fists clenched and unclenched in a rhythm of barely restrained fury, his teeth grinding audibly. But he didn't fire. He wouldn't—not yet.

Noir's attention returned to the screen before him. The Wayfarer loomed larger with each passing second, its massive silhouette gradually dominating the monitor as the scout ship approached. The vessel moved steadily, guided by the autopilot, its course unwavering. But Noir's thoughts drifted elsewhere, his mind tethered to something distant, far from the cold confines of the ship.

A faint sound reached his ears, nearly lost beneath the steady hum of the engines. It was soft, almost spectral, but unmistakable. Someone was crying.

Noir didn't need to turn to know who it was.

Saffron.

The weight of it all pressed down on him, heavy and relentless, as he stared at the monitor. The conflict within him, the choices he'd made, and the rippling consequences that followed. Why was she crying? He had spared a life, yet at what cost?

* * *

Elise Martin leaned casually against the smooth, metallic wall of Noir's captain's quarters. Her holographic form cast a faint, flickering glow in the amber light that filled the room. Unlike Noir's suspended, weightless figure, her projection seemed solid, as though she truly occupied the space. Yet, where she stood was nothing more than an illusion—a remnant of her long-dead self. Her presence was steady and still, while Noir, floating mid-air, clung to the edge of the desk with his fingers. His body swayed slightly, adjusting to the absence of gravity.

The air in the quarters was stale, carrying the faint, metallic tang of recycled oxygen that lingered with every breath. Beyond the silence between them, Noir could hear the distant hum of the ship's engines, a low, ceaseless pulse resonating through the hull. It vibrated in his bones, a reminder of the vast, unending expanse of space outside.

Elise smiled at him—the kind of smile one reserves for an old friend after a long absence. It was warm, perhaps warmer than Noir deserved. But he didn't notice. His eyes were dull, shadowed with guilt, and when he finally spoke, his voice was heavy, as if it had to be dragged from the depths of his chest.

"Great Elise," he began, his tone low and brittle, *"what do you feel like? Did I make a grave mistake? Did I fuck it up?"*

Her expression softened, though she shook her head gently. "No, Noir. You did nothing wrong. You're one of the best human beings I've ever met. Your actions proved that to me."

He swallowed hard, his throat dry despite the artificial air. His lips twitched into the beginnings of a smile, but it faltered, collapsing into something that barely resembled hope. "You don't really mean that," he muttered, his voice laced with quiet defeat. *"You're just saying that to make me feel better, aren't you?"*

Elise chuckled softly, a sound that, even three hundred years after her death, carried the same sharp honesty of someone who rarely indulged in pleasantries. *"Noir, I never said anything to make someone feel better when I was alive. I wasn't in the business of offering false hope. And I certainly don't intend to start now."*

He nodded, but his thoughts were elsewhere. The memory of opening the ship's doors for Humar clawed at him, an unrelenting specter haunting his mind. He saw Saffron's tear-streaked face as she crumbled under the weight of the moment. The tightening in his chest returned, a sharp reminder of the cost of his choices.

"Hearing that makes me feel better, but ever since I let Humar back onto the ship, I've been in constant mental anguish. It doesn't stop. Especially… especially when I keep thinking about Saffron. She cried, Elise. She broke down, and I felt—no, I feel—guilty. And I don't even know why."

Elise's tone shifted, soft and almost maternal. "It's natural, Noir," she said quietly. *"You're dealing with a criminal who's become something beyond human—a cyborg with immense power, a man who lost his morality long before he replaced his flesh with steel. Guilt, fear… they're natural responses when you save someone like that."*

"But why Saffron? Why did she react like that?" Noir's voice cracked, the words tumbling out too fast. The memory of her crumpled, weeping figure clawed at him, dragging him into a strange, unfamiliar dread.

Elise sighed—a long, slow exhale, heavy with unspoken meaning. "Perhaps she sees something you don't. Maybe, as a woman, she anticipates something you cannot."

Noir flinched, his body recoiling ever so slightly in the air. His grip on the desk tightened, and the weightless atmosphere suddenly felt oppressive, suffocating. *"What are you trying to say, Elise?"* he asked, his voice lower now, wary.

Elise held his gaze, her unblinking eyes steady and calm, yet unsettling. *"I'm not saying anything, Noir. But as a woman, I can relate to Saffron. Sometimes, we see things, anticipate things, that men... don't."*

Noir's heart pounded against his ribs, the sound loud in his ears. His mouth was dry, and the recycled air around him felt thin and cold. "What does that mean?" he asked, his voice sharp but strained. "What's going on?"

"Saffron is a beautiful girl, Noir. And Humar is a very lonely man. It doesn't take much to guess what kind of primal urges might drive a man like him."

Noir stared at Elise, his stomach plummeting as her words sank in. His mind spun, the once-familiar air now feeling too cold, too foreign. His throat tightened as though the ability to speak had been stripped from him. After what felt like an eternity, he managed to whisper, his voice hoarse and trembling, *"Elise, you told me to take life as it comes. To not overthink it. I can do that with my own life, but what about Saffron's? What about hers?"*

Elise's gaze didn't waver, her holographic eyes steady and unblinking. She said nothing.

Noir's voice cracked through the stagnant air of the captain's quarters, his body trembling slightly as he floated in weightlessness. "If I had left Humar on that nightmare moon, we'd be safe! I brought that monster onto this ship myself—"

"Yes," Elise replied calmly, nodding with deliberate slowness, her flickering form steady against the cool metallic wall. "And now you have to kill this monster with your own two hands."

Noir flinched, her words striking him like a physical blow. "But… wouldn't that be contradictory? Did I save him just so I could kill him with my own hands?" His voice was raw, hollow, as though the question itself had drained the life from him.

Elise's holographic form flickered faintly, her expression remaining soft yet unyielding. "Perhaps. It might be contradictory by some people's logic. But you can't think about that now, Noir."

He shook his head helplessly, his brow furrowed, frustration etched into every movement. *"But how can I kill him, great Elise? No matter what I hit him with, his body… it just bounces everything back at me! How do you kill something like that?"*

For a long moment, Elise didn't respond. The low hum of the ship filled the silence, blending with the faint, rhythmic pulsing of machinery deep within the vessel. The metallic tang of recycled air hung in every shallow, unsatisfying breath. Finally, she sighed, her voice soft with the weight of something ancient and worn.

"Before I took my vow of nonviolence," she began, her words slow and deliberate, "I was one of the deadliest assassins humanity ever produced. I killed more people than I can count across the universe. Tortured more than I care to remember. I spent my life fighting for

death, not life." Her holographic eyes, cold yet somehow still deeply human, locked onto Noir's. "But I have to apologize to you, Noir. I don't know how to deal with a cyborg like Humar. I don't understand this new world. My knowledge is from a time when technology was primitive compared to what you face now. I'm just… a reflection. I exist only in the hyper mind."

Noir's eyes widened, desperation creeping into his voice as he nearly pleaded. *"But you're Elise Martin! The real Elise Martin! You're the most brilliant human being of all time—"*

Elise let out a short, sharp laugh that echoed in the sterile silence of the quarters. *"That's an exaggeration, Noir. People called me that out of love, not truth. I was just an ordinary human being."*

Noir searched her face, clinging to the last remnants of hope she might offer. His voice dropped to a near whisper. "But what you know, what you understand—you believe it. You believe it's the truth. Please… please tell me what I should do."

Elise paused, her holographic form becoming unnaturally still. For a long moment, she said nothing. The silence felt deafening, the worries of the universe pressing down on Noir as if to fill the void between them. Her gaze lowered to her open palms, her fingers moving faintly over the empty air, as though she could still feel the tactile memory of the blood she once spilled.

"When I worked as an assassin, the prime chancellors of humanity sent me to alien worlds to eliminate their leaders. Most of the time, I had almost no information about my targets. The odds were always against me. But over time, I developed a principle." She lifted her head, her eyes sharp and piercing—like the blades she once wielded. *"Noir, you must turn Humar's greatest advantage into his greatest weakness."*

Noir blinked, astonished. His voice wavered as he tried to hold steady. "How would I even do that?"

Her expression softened, her eyes clouded with something close to sorrow. The corners of her lips twitched, as though they were attempting a sympathetic smile but couldn't quite succeed. *"I don't know, Noir. I can't know. Your world, your technology… it's beyond me. Without a biological body, I can't evolve with it. I'm trapped in a future I can no longer touch. I can't adapt, I can't learn."*

A cold realization seeped into Noir: there was no easy answer, no shortcut, no ready-made solution he could simply apply.

"You have to think," Elise said softly, her voice barely more than a whisper. Her form flickered slightly, faint static breaking across her image. "You must come up with the solution. Because that's what being human is, Noir: adapting, overcoming, even when the odds seem insurmountable."

Noir stared at her, his throat dry, his mind spinning as his grip on the desk loosened slightly. Her words echoed in his ears, leaving him with the suffocating weight of a future he would have to forge without clarity. Outside the ship, the stars blinked indifferently in the abyss of space, cold and apathetic to his struggles. There was no guide, no certainty—just the unyielding truth that the only way forward was through the impossible.

Even long after Elise's image had flickered out of the room, Noir remained motionless, suspended in the same spot. His chest rose and fell with shallow breaths, his hands still clutching the cool edge of the desk as though it could anchor him in the weightlessness. But it didn't. He was adrift, both physically and mentally, overwhelmed by the relentless churn of his thoughts.

What the hell am I supposed to do now? How am I going to turn Humar's greatest strength into his greatest weakness?

The question ricocheted inside Noir's skull, tangling his thoughts like thick, frayed wires sparking under pressure. He clenched his jaw, but the tension in his body refused to ease. His usual coping mechanism—walking to clear his head—nagged at him, an ingrained habit that held no meaning in the zero-gravity environment. Floating offered no solace. It gave his mind no outlet, no semblance of control.

With a frustrated grunt, he shoved off the desk, propelling himself through the corridor like a swimmer cutting through deep water. His body twisted and swayed as he flew toward the gym. The passageways smelled faintly of antiseptic, with the unmistakable tang of recycled oxygen clinging to the air. The walls and surfaces he passed emitted the steady hum of the ship's machinery, a constant, unchanging rhythm that somehow only heightened his agitation.

He needed gravity. He needed the ground beneath his feet.

The gym greeted him with its sterile, metallic glow— a perfect sphere rotating on its axis like a cosmic machine. The instant Noir flicked the control lever, the room whirred to life, the hum of machinery rising as the chamber began to generate artificial gravity. Slowly, the rotation increased, transforming the spherical room into a colossal treadmill, like a hamster wheel built for humanity's struggles in the void. Noir let his body float toward the center of the floor as the pull strengthened, gravity tugging him down, welcoming the weight returning to his limbs.

He stood, stretching his arms wide, feeling blood surge through his veins. The sensation was almost euphoric, grounding him in a way that zero-gravity never could. With the weight came clarity. Noir began to walk, his boots echoing softly against the steel floor.

His mind latched onto the problem like a puzzle demanding to be solved. Humar Danjon: part man, part machine. But what kind of machine?

Noir's thoughts spiraled back to the vault where he'd first encountered Humar. He'd escaped that titanium tomb, even after his body was frozen. No ordinary human could have survived that. But Humar wasn't ordinary. Something was inside him—a cyber-mind embedded in his skull. It had to be. Humar's biological brain might shut down, rendered unconscious, but the machine inside him wouldn't allow it. The cyber-mind would take over.

But how intelligent could it be?

As he paced, Noir's eyes narrowed, his thoughts slicing through the problem with sharp precision. If the cyber-mind is small enough to fit inside his skull, it can't have too much processing power. Overheating would damage his biological brain. The realization struck like an electric jolt. The cyber-mind must be simple, designed only for essential survival tasks—reactive, not creative.

A faint smile tugged at the corner of his mouth, and his pace quickened. *What if I forced Humar into unconsciousness? Forced the cyber-mind to take over, and then...*

Then I could trick it.

Noir's heart pounded as he walked faster, his footsteps growing louder in the chamber. The rotating floor matched his speed, the artificial gravity increasing as the room's axis spun faster. He could feel the satisfying pull on his muscles, the familiar weight pressing down on his bones. His mind raced just as quickly, fueled by the prospect of a solution. *Poison gas? No. Too risky. Anesthetic in his food? Maybe, but Humar's no fool. He's written books on underworld tricks like these.*

Noir's lips twisted into a bitter grin. Of course, it wouldn't be that easy.

The g-force continued to rise as Noir jogged, his feet pounding harder against the floor with each step. His skin buzzed with adrenaline, and in a moment of reckless abandon, he activated his ferrionics. His body thrummed with particles vibrating at a subatomic level, heightening his senses to an almost unbearable degree. Every inch of him felt as though it were forged from iron, each step reverberating through his bones like a seismic wave. He ran faster, the spinning room matching his pace, its speed increasing with his determination.

The gravitational force pressed harder, turning every step into a Herculean effort as his muscles screamed under the strain. The dull thud of his footfalls grew thunderous, echoing against the steel walls. The mechanical hum of the room shifted into a high-pitched whine, the centrifugal force building relentlessly. Noir could feel the weight of his own body intensify, as if he were sinking into an invisible quicksand. His skin crawled with the heavy sensation, sweat beading on his forehead before trickling down his face. A faint metallic tang stung his lips as he gasped for air, his breathing ragged and uneven, the atmosphere thickening around him.

But still, he didn't stop. Just a little faster, a little more…

A red haze edged his vision, but the feverish thrill of pushing himself beyond his limits gripped him with an unrelenting fervor. His body begged him to stop, muscles burning and lungs on fire, but his mind spun faster than the room, faster than his body could follow.

Suddenly, the piercing shriek of an alarm sliced through the air, jarring his senses.

A bright red light flared in the corner of the gym, pulsing in rhythmic urgency. Eni's voice echoed sharply through the intercom, crisp and commanding. "Your Highness Noir! Stop immediately or you will lose consciousness!"

Noir didn't stop.

The gravitational pull felt as though it would crush him. His lungs burned, his legs trembled beneath the immense weight, and yet he pushed harder. Something deep within him—a reckless defiance, a burst of raw emotion— drove him forward. He needed to see how far he could go, how much he could endure, before the universe itself screamed back at him: *enough!*

An electric sensation surged through Noir's body.

He shouted, *"What did you say, Eni?! What did you just say?"*

The disembodied voice of Eni, the hyper-mind AI, responded with cool precision, a stark contrast to Noir's fevered intensity. "I said: Please stop immediately, or you will lose consciousness."

Noir's breath escaped in ragged bursts, the air tasting sharp and metallic on his dry tongue. The crushing pressure around him tightened, inch by inch, as though the ship itself were bearing down on him. "Pass out?" he gasped, his wild eyes darting around the spinning room. "Did you just say I'm going to pass out?"

"Yes," Eni confirmed, her tone as calm and steady as ever.

A wicked grin split across Noir's face—defiant, ferocious. His legs trembled under the mounting force, the gravity pressing against him like a tidal wave. "Eni! I want to see how far I can go without passing out!"

"But why, your highness?" Eni's voice carried the faintest trace of simulated concern, a programmed attempt to mimic human empathy.

"There's a reason," Noir snapped, his jaw clenched so tightly it felt as though his teeth might crack. Sweat streamed down his face, stinging his eyes, but he welcomed the burn. "There's a good reason."

"What is that reason?" Eni asked, her tone smooth, though Noir could almost imagine the AI running endless calculations, searching for logic in his chaos.

"I'll tell you when it's time," Noir growled through labored breaths. His vision blurred at the edges, artificial gravity pounding against his skull like a hydraulic press. *"Now, Eni! Bring me to the deep gravitational forces! Increase the gravity! More! And more! And even more—"*

"But your highness," Eni interrupted, her tone shifting, carrying a subtle edge of artificial alarm. "This is becoming exceedingly dangerous. An unenhanced human cannot survive under the gravitational force you're currently experiencing. Your ferrionics are sustaining you, but without them, you would have been crushed already."

Noir laughed, the sound harsh, raw, almost feral. His voice rasped as his ribs contracted, his lungs struggling to expand against the overwhelming force. The room spun in a distorted blur of steel walls and flashing lights, the gravitational field warping reality around him, pulling at him with the weight of a black hole.

"That's exactly what I want, Eni!" he rasped, his defiance cutting through the air like a blade. *"I want to stand tall in gravity that would flatten others! I want to stay conscious where anyone else would collapse!"*

The hum of the machines deepened, a resonant growl that seemed to mock the limits of his body. Noir's flesh screamed in protest, every fiber straining to keep him upright.

Eni paused, its digital processes whirring silently, calculating the incomprehensible. "I am sorry, your highness," Eni said, its voice laced with something resembling resignation. *"This human behavior is beyond the comprehension of a hyper-mind calculator."*

Noir snarled, his teeth gritted as he pushed forward, defying the force that threatened to crush his very bones. Gravity pulled at his joints, his tendons stretched to their limits, as though they might snap under the strain. "You don't need to understand it, Eni," he growled through clenched teeth. *"You couldn't use the information anyway. Just give me the data from the central unit—every tip, every strategy—to help me stay conscious in this gravitational force."*

His breath came in sharp, ragged bursts, each step forward a monumental effort. The artificial gravity turned his movements into slow, punishing lunges. Every footfall felt like it carried the weight of a collapsing star. His muscles burned with a searing intensity, his heartbeat a frantic drum pounding through his skull.

"I will retrieve all available data," Eni responded evenly. "However, it will take significant time to train an unenhanced human to reach superhuman capacity."

"No time!" Noir roared, his vision narrowing, tunneling into a single point of focus. *"I don't have a microsecond to waste!"*

Eni fell silent. The ship's hum filled the void, a whisper of judgment that seemed to resonate in the space between them. Noir could feel it—the crushing force that should have pulverized him by now, held back only by the ferrionics coursing through his body, thrumming like electrified particles. But it wasn't enough. It would never be enough.

He needed to be more than human. Unyielding. Unbreakable. *For Saffron.*

The thought of her face—beautiful, vulnerable— flashed in his mind, igniting something primal within him. It pushed him forward, past the limits of his endurance. His body screamed in agony, his chest heaving as if every breath were being torn from his lungs. His legs trembled, barely able to hold him upright, as the gravitational force crushed him from all sides, threatening to reduce him to dust.

He grunted, his effort turning into a guttural roar. Saliva mixed with blood trickled from the corner of his mouth, staining his lips with a bitter metallic tang. His tongue tasted copper, sharp and cold, as the monstrous grip of gravity clawed at his bones, unrelenting in its assault.

He had to achieve a strength impossible for a man of flesh and blood. It was the only way to save her.

"I understand," Eni said, its voice finally yielding, carrying a tone that almost resembled reluctant submission. "I will provide my assistance."

* * *

After a long sleep that felt like slipping through layers of soft, dark oblivion, Noir awoke. His body was slowly stitching itself back together from the punishment of the gravity training. The soreness lingered in his muscles, a dull ache that refused to fade. But he had more pressing concerns than the pain. He had to find Saffron.

The ship's corridors were eerily silent, the hum of the engines a low, persistent drone beneath his feet. Invisible to most, Noir could feel the ship accelerating through the void. His ferrionics were attuned to every subtle shift in velocity. A neutron star loomed ahead, its immense gravitational field beginning to distort their trajectory. Though still just a tiny, imperceptible speck in the distance, it exerted a pull that even Noir's enhanced senses could not ignore.

He found Saffron in one of the most isolated corners of the ship, lying beside a massive round window, her silhouette framed by the vast expanse of space.

Stars glittered like diamond dust scattered across the endless black, and beyond them, a nebula unfurled a sprawling bloom of gas and light, swirling in colors that defied description. It was bizarre, beautiful, and utterly indifferent to the lives observing from the cold metal shell of the ship.

Noir slowed his pace, his boots making soft, rhythmic thuds against the floor. There was something fragile about the way she lay there, still and silent, staring out into the infinite. He hesitated, his chest tightening. This wasn't the Saffron he knew—the fierce, intelligent woman whose fire burned so brightly. This was someone else. Someone caught in the gravitational pull of something deeper. Something that terrified him.

"Saffron?" Noir called softly as he came to stand beside her, his voice barely louder than the distant hum of the ship.

She didn't turn to face him fully. Instead, she shifted her head slightly, her profile stark against the shimmering nebula. The stars reflected in her eyes, giving them an otherworldly glow. But there was no warmth there—only a cold, distant emptiness. She remained silent, the space between them stretching like a vast, unbridgeable chasm.

Noir tried to force a smile, but it felt wrong, like a mask that didn't fit. *"You're really angry at me, aren't you?"*

Her lips remained sealed, the tension in her jaw betraying the storm of emotions simmering just beneath the surface.

A wave of guilt washed over Noir, deep and allconsuming, gnawing at his thoughts like an unrelenting parasite. He opened his mouth, but the words felt clumsy, inadequate. "I just wanted to have a little chat with you, Saffron. If that's alright."

She finally looked at him—really looked at him— and when she did, her eyes were wide, her face pulled into a strange, eerie smile that sent a shiver down Noir's spine. Her voice, when it came, was cold and mocking. *"What does a great saint like you have to say to an insignificant madriel like me?"*

Noir blinked, taken aback. "What are you saying, Saffron?"

Her lips twisted into a bitter sneer. *"Why? Am I wrong?"* Her voice rose, sharp and cutting, each word a blade. "You're different from the men I know. You're busy with the big, important issues of the universe. You're ready to toss aside a madriel like me—just trash, unrecyclable—so the cosmic beasts don't get the wrong idea about humans."

Her words hit Noir like a blow to the gut. He staggered inwardly, his mind reeling from the force of her accusation. "Why are you saying this, Saffron?"

"Did I say something wrong? Of course I did." She laughed bitterly, the sound harsh and brittle, like glass shattering in the silence. *"I'm just an insignificant, ignorant, illiterate woman. How could I ever hope to understand the great mysteries of the universe? No, I can't—"*

"Saffron, please—" Noir's voice cracked, raw with desperation.

But she turned away from him, her gaze locking onto the endless expanse beyond the window. The nebula swirled in the distance, a chaotic bloom of gas and light, indifferent to the pain inside the ship. "Leave me alone, Noir. I beg you."

Her words cut deeper than a knife. "Please, Saffron," he pleaded, his voice barely above a whisper. "I need to talk to you."

"No." Her voice was firm, final, and unyielding. Her head shook slowly, deliberately, as though it was the only way to keep herself from unraveling. *"There's nothing left to say. Please… just leave me alone."*

Noir's heart twisted painfully as he watched her rub at her eyes, determined not to let a single tear fall. She was shutting him out, closing herself off entirely, and it tore at him like nothing else could. The spirited, fierce woman he had always known now seemed broken in a way that made him feel utterly powerless.

He swallowed the lump in his throat and turned away.

I'm a criminal, he thought bitterly. No better than the space pirate terrorizing the ship. Maybe worse.

Noir stepped into the dimly lit control room, where the faint hum of the ship's machinery served as a constant backdrop to the oppressive silence. Humar sat hunched before the control panel, his shoulders slumped, his face tight with worry. The shifting glow of the monitors bathed his features in alternating hues of blue and orange, casting sharp shadows that deepened the lines etched across his brow. His fingers tapped lightly on the edge of the panel, a subconscious twitch betraying his unease.

As Noir's boots clicked against the metal floor, Humar's head turned slowly, his eyes narrowing with a calculating coldness. Yet beneath the hardened veneer, something else flickered—distress, perhaps.

"Noir," Humar said, his voice flat, devoid of its usual bravado. "I need to have a word with you."

Noir's gaze flicked to the compact automatic gun strapped to Humar's waist, its sleek black surface gleaming under the dim light like a grim promise of violence. He stopped just short of the control panel, his posture loose, almost casual, though his eyes remained sharp. "What do you want?"

Humar exhaled through his nose, the sound long and heavy. His lips pressed into a thin line as though swallowing a bitter truth.

"I really wanted my crew back," he muttered, his voice tinged with regret. "I thought I could get them back from that moon in the dwarf star system."

Noir tilted his head slightly, his voice measured. *"Yes, I'm aware."*

"But as you can see," Humar gestured vaguely toward the vast emptiness beyond the viewports, "I failed. Miserably. Not only were they dead, but their corpses… they nearly killed me." His voice dropped, a tremor of despair cutting through the usual edge. "Do you know what that means?"

Noir's expression remained impassive. "You want to assemble a new crew."

Humar flinched, his eyes widening for just a moment before narrowing into icy slits. He hadn't expected Noir to be so blunt, so perceptive. For a long moment, they locked eyes, tension crackling between them like static in the air.

"Yes," Humar said at last, his voice cold and measured. "I'll have to rebuild. And I'll need new people."

Noir's lips twisted into a sneer, his tone laced with mocking disdain. "New people? No, what you really need are monsters like yourself."

Humar's expression hardened, his jaw clenching visibly. The grinding of his teeth was faint but audible as he fixed Noir with a fierce glare. "Sometimes, I'm amazed at how defiant you are," he spat. "Do you know what kind of people display that level of defiance?"

"I do," Noir replied, his voice calm but sharp.

"Oh, do you now?" Humar's tone dripped with sarcasm. "Then enlighten me."

"Two types of people," Noir said smoothly. *"Those who are brave, and those who are idiots. I'm not a brave person, so I must be an idiot."*

The corner of Noir's mouth lifted into a grin, but it failed to elicit any reaction from Humar. Instead, the cyborg's face darkened further, the lines around his mouth deepening as he spoke slowly, deliberately. *"Noir, you are anything but an idiot. And that's precisely why I've decided to recruit you."*

Noir's blood ran cold. A sudden, creeping dread seeped into his bones. He stared at Humar in disbelief, his mind struggling to process the words. Is this bastard joking with me? "Recruit me? Why?"

Humar's smile was thin and humorless, more of a grim slash across his face. *"You think it's impossible, don't you? That a ferrionic man with principles—a man of integrity—could join my crew. But this isn't what you think it is."*

Noir's brow furrowed, suspicion knitting his expression. "What do you mean?"

Humar's eyes gleamed with a dark, twisted light. There was something almost predatory in his gaze, like a hunter cornering its prey. *"In the twentieth century, on Old Earth, scientists made an interesting discovery about human biology. The frontal lobe of the brain—do you know what that controls?"*

Noir didn't answer, but a knot of unease tightened in his gut.

"Morality," Humar said, the word a near-hiss as it left his lips. "And I've found a way to... liberate people from it."

Noir's eyes widened, horror dawning as Humar continued, his voice disturbingly steady, like a lecturer explaining the obvious. *"I've developed a device—the Transfabriel Ultra Liberator. It targets the neurons responsible for morality and fries them. Once done, you're free. Free from your absurd notions of right and wrong. Free to do what needs to be done."*

Noir felt a chill crawl up his spine. The way Humar spoke—so matter-of-fact, so devoid of any sense of horror— was more disturbing than the words themselves.

"Free?" Noir echoed, his voice barely above a whisper, each syllable strained with disbelief.

"Yes," Humar replied, his tone dark and weighted with conviction. *"You'll be able to kill without hesitation, without remorse. Man, woman, child—it won't matter. You'll be free of guilt, free of the chains that hold you back."*

Noir's mouth felt dry, his thoughts spinning wildly as he tried to grasp the full magnitude of what Humar was proposing. This wasn't just an invitation to join his crew; it was a complete and irreversible violation of his very humanity—a mutilation of everything he was.

Humar leaned back, his posture almost casual, his eyes scanning Noir with the detached precision of a surgeon selecting where to make the first cut. "The device is painless," he continued, as though that detail somehow softened the horror of it. "It scans your brain, pinpoints the target region, and drills—just a small puncture. You'll heal in a day. And then, you'll be a new man."

A smile crept across Humar's face, warm and almost fatherly. But to Noir, it was the smile of a predator—a beast wearing the guise of kindness. Noir couldn't move, couldn't speak. His heart pounded in his chest, each beat like a hammer striking the walls of his ribcage, deafening in the suffocating silence.

Humar, mistaking Noir's frozen terror for mere hesitation, shook his head slowly. "I know it sounds terrifying," he said, his voice softening as though he were comforting a frightened child. *"But once you've gone through with it, you'll see how easy life becomes. You'll finally be free."*

Noir remained motionless, his mind a storm of fear, disbelief, and a creeping sense of inevitability. He could feel Humar's inhuman gaze drilling into him, weighing him, calculating. This wasn't a choice—it was a trap, a noose tightening around his neck.

Freedom from morality.

The terrifying phrase echoed in Noir's mind, hollow and relentless, like the whisper of a malevolent specter.

The room seemed colder now, the air heavier, as though the very atmosphere had absorbed the weight of Humar's words. Noir's skin prickled with a visceral fear that clawed up his spine, leaving him tense and trembling. But beneath the fear, lurking like a shadow at the edge of his consciousness, was something far worse—a flicker of understanding. There was a dark, primal logic to what Humar was saying. And that flicker, that faint resonance, was what terrified Noir most of all.

It wasn't just Humar's plan that horrified him—it was the small, treacherous part of himself that almost understood. And that, more than anything, made Noir feel sick to his very core.

"That's enough prologue. Let's get to business." Humar's voice slithered like oil, slick and unnerving, as he licked his blackish-red lips, the wet sheen catching the dim light of the cabin. He sighed deeply, the sound resonating like the hiss of the ship's engines, his eyes dropping to study his nails with a strange mix of casual indifference and sinister intent. Then he looked up, locking his gaze onto Noir with an intensity that felt like a vice tightening.

His dark, tired eyes carried an eerie sadness, an emptiness tinged with something far more disturbing than mere loneliness. *"Noir,"* he murmured, his tone soft but laden with an unsettling weight, *"I am a very lonely man. I've been imprisoned for so long. A man has his needs, you understand?"* The air grew heavy, the tension in his words spreading like a toxic mist, impossible to ignore. "All my female crew members... dead, gone. Now, I'm without a partner."

Noir's chest tightened, his stomach twisting into knots, but his face remained a mask of cold, controlled calm. His heartbeat thundered in his ears, but he dared not let even a flicker of emotion show.

Humar's lips curled into a grin—wide, unsettling, and predatory—his teeth glinting faintly. *"I really like that madriel girl you have aboard,"* he said, his words drawn out, savoring every syllable. *"And her name is so... charming."* He paused, letting the name roll off his tongue like a poisoned dagger. *"Saffron."*

Noir's jaw clenched, his teeth grinding together as a flash of white-hot anger burned beneath the surface. His fingers flexed ever so slightly at his sides, itching for something to grip, something to break.

"I've decided," Humar continued, leaning closer, his presence invasive despite the physical distance. The musky stench of his unwashed, hybrid body mingled with the ship's sterile air, nauseating in its potency. *"Saffron will be my new partner."* His eyebrows twitched in a grotesque dance of mockery. *"What do you think?"*

Noir met Humar's gaze with unflinching indifference. "You have the personality of a monster," he said, his voice laced with biting sarcasm. "So, it kind of fits."

Humar's expression darkened instantly. His pupils flared wide, the red glow in his eyes intensifying as his nostrils flared like a predator ready to strike. In a single, fluid motion, he yanked the compact blaster from his waist, leveling it at Noir. The weapon buzzed softly, the barrel's faint red glow bathing Humar's face in an ominous light. "Listen, Noir," Humar hissed, his voice cold and venomous, "I'm telling you this for your own good. You're skating on very thin ice. Cross that line, and I won't even give you a chance to regret it."

Noir didn't flinch. Instead, the barest flicker of amusement ghosted across his face. "But you wanted to know what I think—"

"I didn't ask!" Humar roared, his voice reverberating harshly in the confined space. His grip tightened on the blaster, his knuckles whitening. *"I wasn't looking for your opinion! I was telling you what I'm going to do. That's it!"* His chest heaved with rage as he took a long, deliberate breath, forcing his composure back into place. The effort to rein himself in only seemed to amplify the manic energy in his eyes. "Do you know what your problem is?"

"I will," Noir replied, his tone dry and razor-sharp, *"as soon as you tell me."*

Humar snarled, jabbing the barrel of the blaster toward him, the motion punctuating his words. "No, you couldn't possibly know. You're stuck in that old era. Elise Martin's era of right and wrong, crime and greatness, outdated ideas that mean nothing anymore!" His voice rose, shrill and volatile, tinged with a manic fervor that bordered on unhinged. "This is the modern age! A single, tiny piece of your brain decides what's moral and what's not. But what if someone doesn't have that part? Can you blame them? Can you call them a criminal?"

Noir said nothing, his expression carefully neutral, though he could feel the heat of Humar's rage radiating off him like steam from a boiling pot. There was no reasoning with a lunatic, no arguing with a gun-waving tyrant who happened to be the most feared figure in recent history. Humar didn't debate; he dictated. Noir's words would never matter to someone like him.

"In Elise Martin's ancient world, criminals and men of principle existed," Humar continued, his voice lowering, eyes narrowing. "But now, none of that matters. Morality is a relic." He straightened, his gaze sharp and cruel. *"Take Saffron, for example. Do you think, just because I like her, I'd force myself on her like some low-down rapist?"* Noir stared, unblinking.

"Of course not," Humar barked, almost incredulous. *"I'm not some monster. I'm a man of logic."* He placed a hand on his chest, feigning nobility. "I'll simply make a small adjustment in her brain. She'll see me differently after that, Noir. She'll want me. Desperately. Like an insect drawn to a flame, like an asteroid locked in the pull of a black hole." He grinned, wide and grotesque. *"Do you understand?"*

Noir nodded, the movement measured and deliberate. *"I understand completely."*

At that moment, the ship trembled—subtle, almost imperceptible, but there. Humar's brow furrowed, his eyes darting toward Noir. "What the hell was that?"

"We've entered the gravitational pull of the neutron star," Noir answered calmly. *"Our velocity is accelerating exponentially. The ship's body is beginning to vibrate under extreme faster-than-light speeds. We'll use the star's gravity to slingshot out of the region."*

Humar's expression shifted, intrigued. "The slingshot effect? Using gravitational forces to boost the velocity?"

"Exactly."

"Highly unstable."

"A little."

Humar's gaze darkened. "And if you've miscalculated?"

"We'll crash into the star," Noir replied flatly. *"But I haven't."*

Humar glared, then, with a sharp push, propelled himself upward. His anti-grav thrusters engaged with a low whine, guiding him back down to the control panel. "Damn this weightless environment," he muttered, his voice echoing faintly. *"Spin the ship, Noir. I want gravity back. I don't care about fuel conservation."*

Noir's lips twitched. "Whatever you say."

As the ship's engines hummed louder, Noir's gaze flickered toward Humar's back. Outside the viewport, the stars stretched into elongated streaks, blurred by their increasing velocity. The neutron star's faint glow bathed the control room in long, shifting shadows. The moral dilemma, the fate of Saffron, the ship, the cargo—all of it teetered on a fragile axis, balanced between survival and control.

The panels before Noir blinked and flickered, streams of alien constellations and raw data charting the ship's precarious course near the neutron star. The soft, blue glow of the holo-map illuminated his face as he studied the projected route, his fingers tracing the shimmering pathways of celestial bodies. The ship's antimatter engines hummed— a quiet, almost ominous sound. Though the Wayfarer carried one of the most advanced fuel systems in the known universe, every microgram had to be rationed with precision. The detour forced upon them by Humar had changed everything.

Now, the ship couldn't rely on its warp drives alone. Twin supermassive black holes lurked ahead like silent predators, bending space itself, making traditional jumps impossible. Instead, they had to ride the gravitational currents of neutron stars and gas giants, slingshotting their way forward. A risky maneuver. One miscalculation, and they'd be crushed, scattered into the void.

Noir's gaze sharpened as he scrutinized the ship's velocity readouts. The hypermind's calculations were flawless, yet something in his gut refused to settle. The Wayfarer wasn't just any ship—it carried life, unique artifacts from across the galaxy, and, above all, Saffron. He couldn't afford any errors. He had to be sure.

The deep pull of the neutron star's gravity was already gripping them, distorting time, drawing them closer. The ship shuddered, metallic groans reverberating through its structure. Noir's arm hairs stood on end—a sign of the increasing electromagnetic radiation bleeding through the hull. Time was slipping through his fingers.

Leaving the control panel, he exhaled slowly, the weight of responsibility pressing into him. The ship, the passengers, Saffron—they were all in his hands.

In the gym, Noir engaged the gravity generator. The whirring intensified, a mechanical hum rising as the room slowly spun. His boots clanged against the reinforced metal floor as the gravitational force surged. With every passing second, the invisible weight grew heavier, pressing down on his muscles, forcing his breath into shorter, labored exhales. The red haze of exertion danced at the edges of his vision. Sweat beaded along his brow, trickling down in slow motion—each droplet feeling as though it were being dragged to its doom.

The rotation of the outer shell blurred into a dizzying vortex, and the crushing pressure gnawed at his bones, threatening to snap them like brittle glass. Noir activated his ferrionics, and a surge of charged particles flooded his limbs, reinforcing his cellular structure against the overwhelming force.

"Your Highness, Noir," Eni's voice rang cool and sharp in his ear.

He exhaled through clenched teeth. "What is it, Eni?"

"You are crossing the safety threshold again."

"I know. I'm doing it on purpose."

"I still fail to understand why." There was a pause, the AI's synthetic voice tinged with something eerily close to concern.

"You'll understand when it's time. Right now, I need you to listen carefully."

Another pause, brief but weighted, as though Eni was recalibrating to the sudden shift in Noir's tone. "Yes, Your Highness?"

"No one else can hear this conversation, correct?"

"No one, Your Highness."

Noir inhaled deeply, his ribs straining against the artificial gravity, lungs burning as if they were being compressed by an unseen vice. His voice came low, deliberate, his vision narrowing at the edges. *"I am issuing a seventh-degree emergency order."*

A silence followed, stretching into an unnatural stillness. Then, in a tone that wavered with rare hesitation, Eni spoke. "A seventh-degree order? Your Highness, are you certain?"

"One hundred percent sure."

"For your information, such an order could push the Wayfarer to the brink of destruction."

"I know, Eni. As captain, it's my authority."

"But why?" This time, the AI's voice carried an uncharacteristic trace of incredulity.

Noir's hands clenched at his sides, sweat stinging his eyes as his body fought against the brutal pull of the artificial gravity. "Humar Danjon intends to perform surgery on Saffron." The words left his lips like a death sentence. *"He plans to make her his... slave."*

"I am aware. It is a tragic decision." Eni's voice remained neutral, as though simply logging a fact.

Noir's heartbeat thundered in his ears. "If he begins that operation, Eni... I want you to execute the order immediately. But if he doesn't, you will delete it."

A long, weighted silence filled the space, stretching into eternity.

Then, at last, Eni spoke.

"And what, precisely, does this order entail?"

Noir's grip tightened against the wall as he pulled himself forward, his muscles trembling under the crushing G-force. *"Decrease the velocity of the Wayfarer."*

"That would require engaging the engines to counter the gravitational forces," Eni responded evenly.

"I'm giving you permission to do so."

Eni's voice softened, as though considering the weight of the command. "Decreasing velocity near the neutron star will almost certainly result in the ship being pulled into its event horizon."

"That's right," Noir said through clenched teeth. *A spectacular way to commit suicide.*

"Do you wish to die, Your Highness?"

Noir let out a harsh breath. "No, I don't. But sometimes… there are things you have to do, even if they destroy you."

Silence stretched between them, thick and heavy, as though Eni was running every possible simulation, mapping out countless paths toward equally bleak outcomes. "Do you truly wish to proceed?"

"Yes, Eni. I do."

Another pause. "Then I will need precise data from you."

Noir could feel his body weakening under the relentless pull of artificial gravity, his muscles screaming for relief, but his mind remained razor-sharp, fueled by a purpose darker than the void outside. He pulled himself across the spinning gym, each movement a brutal exertion. Drawing breath was a battle, speaking was a war.

Life. Death. Injustice. Sacrifice. They were tangled together, indistinguishable. And Noir understood that in this moment, he was about to cross a threshold from which there might be no return—a line he had never dared approach before.

But if it meant saving Saffron from Humar's monstrous grasp?

Then he would cross it.

Without remorse.

Without hesitation.

CHAPTER 8

THE SUICIDE ORDER

The Wayfarer's lights flickered as the gravity generator roared to life, sending a deep hum pulsing through the ship. Noir's stomach dropped, his muscles locking as he felt the first real pull of gravity anchoring him to the deck. The shift was both jarring and reassuring after countless hours adrift in weightlessness.

The ship groaned in protest as artificial gravity wrestled with the distant neutron star's relentless pull, its immense force sending fresh tremors through the hull like muffled thunder. The sharp tang of overheated metal and engine coolant thickened the air, and Noir swore he could feel the ship itself—its stressed bulkheads and straining framework—resonating in his bones. Bracing himself, he moved to the control panel, fingers gliding over the keys with the precision of instinct and repetition. The hypermind's calculations scrolled across the screen in rapid succession, casting flickering light across his face. A thin sheen of sweat chilled his forehead, but he blocked out the shuddering beneath his feet, his focus narrowing to the data in front of him.

The neutron star's blinding white light bled through the viewport, carving stark, shifting shadows along the walls in time with the ship's subtle tremors. But something else sliced through the low hum of the engines—a sound that did not belong. Footsteps.

Noir's fingers froze over the keys. He turned sharply from the panel.

Humar entered with a soldier's precision, his stride measured, his silhouette ominous under the ship's harsh lighting. Two men followed close behind, each gripping Saffron's arms with ironclad force. Her face was flushed, frantic—eyes wide with unfiltered fear.

Noir's gaze sharpened as he took in the two men, noting the identical scars carved into their foreheads, glistening like crude brands. Humar's handiwork, no doubt.

"What the hell is going on here?" Noir demanded, his voice cracking through the tension like a gunshot.

Humar's lips curled into a thin, icy smile. "Nothing that concerns you, Captain." His tone cut through the space between them like a monomolecular blade. "Meet Darin and Fein." He gestured to his subordinates with an air of twisted pride. *"They were once part of the Galactic Police Force, but now—"* his grin stretched, predatory, *"they serve me. Without question."*

Noir's stomach twisted, the acidic burn of disgust creeping up his throat as he registered the vacant sheen in their eyes, the eerie compliance. This wasn't loyalty. This was something worse. Humar had turned them into husks of what they once were. Puppets.

Noir's hands curled into fists, nails digging into his palms as he looked at the once-proud officers, now reduced to little more than vessels drained of will.

"What the hell have you done to them?" he spat, forcing steel into his voice.

Humar exhaled a mock sigh, feigning boredom. *"Ah, nothing too strenuous. They're simply going to prep Saffron for a little procedure in the medbay."* His words dripped with false nonchalance, but the glint in his eye made Noir's pulse spike.

Saffron's struggles intensified. She twisted, thrashed against the crushing grip of Darin and Fein, but they didn't budge—genetically enhanced strength turning her resistance into a futile effort. Her gaze locked onto Noir's, pleading, desperate, her voice cutting through the stale air like a razor.

"Noir! Save me! Please!"

The helplessness in her voice sent a jagged bolt through Noir's chest, leaving a raw wound in its wake. His stance shifted, rage coiling tight in his muscles as he took a sharp step forward. His voice was a growl, low and lethal.

"Let. Her. Go."

Darin and Fein exchanged a look, then sneered. Their laughter was jagged, grating—ricocheting off the cold metal walls like some sick, discordant melody.

Humar merely watched, his twisted smirk deepening, savoring the moment like a master pulling the strings of his marionettes.

Noir's voice sharpened like a honed blade as he growled, "Humar has stolen your free will. He's twisted your minds, made you his slaves! Can't you see what he's done?"

The men didn't flinch. Darin raised a hand to his scar as if it were a badge of honor, his expression disturbingly serene. *"If he altered us, he did it for our own good,"* he replied, his voice chillingly empty. Fein nodded beside him, echoing, *"He did it for us."*

Their eyes were hollow, stripped of the fire that once drove them as enforcers of justice. They were no longer men—only remnants, puppets carved to reflect Humar's will. Noir felt the weight of the moment pressing down on him, a gravitational force threatening to crush him under its merciless grip. Humar's twisted creation stood before him— free will stolen, morality sliced apart by the cold precision of a scalpel.

Saffron's cry jolted him back to the present, her voice raw with desperation.

As Darin and Fein dragged her toward the exit, her screams echoed behind, a sound that clawed its way into Noir's chest. Humar only shook his head, muttering, *"Such a naïve little creature,"* his tone so dismissive it made Noir's stomach churn.

Every instinct in Noir screamed for blood, urging him to tear Humar apart piece by piece. His gaze darkened, seething with a rage that only deepened Humar's amusement. For a heartbeat, their eyes locked—two opposing forces poised for a collision, every muscle in Noir's body primed for a fight.

Humar's expression shifted, his cold amusement hardening into a predator's calm. "Careful, Noir," he said, his voice smooth and lethal. *"You're sharp enough to know better than to defy me. I have biotron shields embedded in my body. A single blaster shot will only ricochet back at you."*

Noir's jaw tightened as he forced himself to stay silent, controlled fury simmering beneath the surface.

Humar's face twisted into an almost affectionate smile, but there was nothing human in it. "You're valuable to me, Noir. Once my work is complete, we'll command the Xenosys region together.

Saffron, you, and I—bound by a force no one can withstand. So don't do anything… foolish."

Noir gave him nothing in return, his silence a deliberate act of defiance. But beneath the stillness, his mind was a storm of calculations, contingencies, and an unyielding resolve that refused to break.

Humar's mocking grin returned, his tone taunting. *"What's wrong, Noir? Cat got your tongue?"*

Noir's eyes narrowed, his voice low and venomous. "Go to hell, Humar."

His words ignited a flicker of rage in Humar's gaze. For a fraction of a second, the mask slipped, revealing the raw, feral thing lurking beneath. But just as quickly, his control snapped back into place, his expression cooling with an eerie finality.

A shiver ran up Noir's spine as Humar leaned in, his voice a quiet venom. "Hell is where I am, Captain. And it's exactly where I plan to take you."

The Wayfarer trembled, its hull groaning like a man stepping into the heart of a blizzard. Noir steadied himself against the control panel, gripping its metal edge as if anchoring himself against the ship's distress. His eyes darted over the indicators—one red dot flared briefly, pulsing a silent warning before vanishing.

Beneath his boots, the deck vibrated with a restless energy, the ship's engines thrumming like a caged beast, its metallic veins carrying the deep, unsettled hum of imminent danger. They were perilously close to the neutron star. Noir's seventh-degree order was in effect. Velocity dropping. The Wayfarer inching closer to the event horizon—a point of no return.

Humar turned, his glare laced with scorn. *"What the hell is going on, Captain?"*

Noir met his gaze, expression smooth but edged with quiet defiance. "We're nearing the neutron star. Adjusting our course to keep the ship from being torn apart." His tone carried the weight of command, leaving no room for debate, but he could see the suspicion gleaming in Humar's eyes.

"Whether you like it or not," Noir added, his voice sharp, *"I am still the ship's captain. You'll have to trust me with this."*

Humar paused, his eyes dissecting Noir as if searching for any flaw, any weakness. But finally, with a grunt, he turned and continued down the corridor toward the med bay, where Darin and Fein had likely already restrained Saffron.

Noir exhaled, his gaze snapping back to the controls. The numbers on the screen traced their slow descent, the ship creeping ever closer to the neutron star's relentless pull. Each tremor from the engines pulsed through the control room, a deep, foreboding groan that sent a shiver down his spine. The cold metal of the control panel pressed against his fingertips, the bitter tang of anxiety sharp on his tongue as he watched their course drift further into the gravity well. If this trajectory remained unchecked, the Wayfarer would breach the event horizon, its fate sealed in the crushing embrace of the neutron star's gravity.

The game had begun, and Noir's move was already in motion. Rising from his seat, he felt the weight of his decision settling over him, a cold specter of dread whispering at the edges of his mind. There was no turning back now. With measured steps, he retraced his path down the corridor toward the med bay.

He arrived at the doors, where a red warning light pulsed insistently, forbidding entry. Noir punched in his captain's code, and the doors hissed open.

The operating chamber unfolded before him—pristine, sterile, its acrid antiseptic scent laced with the faint trace of something metallic. The overhead lights emitted a low buzz, casting an unyielding white glare over the stark interior.

At the center of it all, Saffron lay restrained on the operating bed. A luminous white ring hovered just above her forehead, like a synthetic halo pulsing with eerie light against her skin. Holographic lines of coded text rippled above her in shifting projections, the neurometer calibrating its parameters as data streamed in fluid pulses. Shadows flickered over her still face, her expression caught between defiance and something quieter—an unsettling calm that softened her gaze as she locked eyes with Noir.

Humar's face split into a grin as he noticed Noir's arrival. He gestured with exaggerated enthusiasm, his voice bright with mock cheer. *"Ah, Noir! Perfect timing. We'll need your assistance here."*

Noir's response was as cold as the steel beneath his feet. "Why would you think I'd help you in any way?"

"Oh, you won't need to lift a finger." Humar chuckled, his voice slick with satisfaction. *"Saffron has a… fondness for you, after all. See, when she looks at you, certain regions in her brain react. And we, well, we'll be isolating those regions."* His tone was light, but the undercurrent of anticipation in his words carried a sinister weight.

A dark fury coiled within Noir. "You're planning to destroy them."

Humar's eyes gleamed with perverse delight. "Precisely."

One of the two officers—Darin, perhaps, or Fein— spoke up, holding a gas mask in one hand, poised to administer it at Humar's command. Noir could barely tell them apart anymore; they had become mere extensions of Humar's will, lifeless tools in his arsenal.

"Captain," the twin said, barely containing his excitement, "the neurometer's picking up a signal."

"Perfect!" Humar crowed, clapping his hands. His gaze slid back to Noir, his grin widening into something almost grotesque. *"Come closer, would you? Just a bit closer to dear Saffron here."*

Reluctantly, Noir stepped forward, placing a hand on Saffron's. The chill of her skin sent a jolt through him, but her grip was steady. She looked up at him, her face pale yet composed, a faint smile playing on her lips.

"Noir," she murmured, her voice barely above a whisper, "I figured it out. I know why you did what you did. You don't have to be sorry."

The bitterness in his chest sharpened into something jagged. "Saffron, I—"

"You had to." Her voice was soft, steady, like the hum of a distant engine. *"There's horror in the universe, injustice... but to fight it, there must be truth. Real justice. You can't defeat the darkness by becoming it."*

"I was mad at you, Noir. I thought you'd sacrificed me to him." Her gaze drifted past Noir to Humar, her expression unyielding. *"But even here, restrained on this bed, I know now—I'm more than what he could take from me. The good in me, my compassion, my sense of justice... that's who I am. Not this body, not these impulses he's so eager to distort. Whatever he tries to create, it won't be me."*

Her smile was radiant, a quiet defiance pulsing beneath it. It carried a warmth that felt like a balm, something pure against the sterile bleakness of the room. It was a farewell smile, one that reached deeper than words.

Humar let out a burst of unchecked glee. "Ah, magnificent, Saffron! Your brain's lighting up like a supernova. My neurometer has mapped every target zone, thanks to you, Noir!"

He gestured to Fein, who stepped forward, securing the gas mask over her face.

As the gas hissed and her eyes began to flutter shut, she looked up at Noir, her smile lingering. *"Goodbye, Noir. The person who wakes up… she won't be me. Forgive her, please."*

Noir felt his chest tighten as he held her hand, her grip weakening. *"Sleep, Saffron,"* he said, his voice rough. "I promise, no one will erase what you are."

Her hand slipped from his, falling limply to her side as she drifted into unconsciousness. The machines around her whirred, their rhythms steady, indifferent to the silent war unfolding in the room. As Noir stood, a crushing weight pressed down on him, his senses sharpening to the ship's tremors—the star's deadly gravity inching closer with every passing moment. The hull groaned under the strain, filling the silence Saffron had left behind. It wasn't just metal and circuits creaking under pressure; it was as if the Wayfarer itself was wailing for her.

Noir exhaled a quiet sigh and straightened, his gaze locking onto Humar's hard, narrowed eyes. Humar's voice was cold steel. "I thought you didn't give false assurances."

Noir's expression remained unmoved. "I don't."

"Then why promise her that no one could take her humanity?"

Noir's face was grim, his words edged with finality.

"Because she'll die before that happens."

A flicker of unease crossed Humar's face. *"What?"*

"Not just her. You, me, and every mindless drone you call crew. We're all dying today."

Disbelief flickered through Humar's eyes, but he smothered it with a sneer. "Yeah, right. You don't have the guts to take down an Etherean-class ship with us on board."

"Oh, but I do." Noir's voice dropped, low and calm, carrying the weight of truth.

Humar's face contorted in a flash of rage and fear. *"Why?"*

Noir gestured toward Saffron, something unreadable flickering in his eyes. "There's a purity in her, a goodness that deserves to be protected. Better she dies human than be twisted into something monstrous."

Humar's cheeks burned crimson with anger. *"Are you out of your damn mind? You'd destroy a priceless ship for… for a nobody?"*

"A human being is never insignificant." Noir's voice took on a sharper edge, each word a scalpel cutting through the air. *"I saved a monster like you, didn't I? Compared to you, Saffron's practically divine. Destroying a ship or two means nothing if it keeps her soul intact."*

With a snarl, Humar seized Noir's collar, his voice rising into a scream of frustration. "You're lying! You're lying!"

Noir's expression remained unshaken. *"You know I don't lie."*

A sharp voice cut through the tension as Darin and Fein echoed, *"Boss, what now?"*

Humar's grip slackened, his fingers trembling as he stared into Noir's cold, unwavering gaze. Noir's eyes burned with something primal, something lethal. "You're forcing a good man to go mad. Be careful, Humar."

Something in Humar's gaze flickered—recognition, horror. For the first time, Noir saw real, unfiltered fear in him. Humar staggered back as though confronted by some creeping, deadly force. But before he could speak, the floor convulsed beneath them. A deep, grinding groan echoed from the ship's core, a metallic wail reverberating through the walls, as if the *Wayfarer* itself rebelled against its impending fate.

The ship buckled violently. Darin's voice rang out in panic. "Captain! This whole place is coming apart!"

Humar's face drained of color as he snapped from his frozen stance. *"Control room. Now!"* He bolted from the chamber, Darin and Fein at his heels, leaving Noir alone with the unconscious Saffron.

Noir knelt beside her, his fingers grazing her cheek. His voice was barely a whisper. *"Sleep well, Saffron. I'll save you. Or die trying."*

With steely determination, Noir slipped a pair of space masks into his clothes and sprinted toward the control room, knowing the time for his final move had arrived. As he entered, Humar's glare met him like a blade, seething with fury.

"You fucking lunatic!" Humar spat.

Noir shrugged. *"Do you believe me now? The Wayfarer is doomed."*

"No!" Humar's voice cracked with desperation. "I'll save it! I'll save my ship!"

"You'll fail."

"Shut up!" Humar barked, turning his attention to the control panel. His fingers flew across the interface with relentless precision, scrambling to override Noir's command. He pushed the twin engines to their limits, setting them for an emergency thrust powerful enough to rip the ship from the neutron star's gravitational chokehold. The G-force would be catastrophic, but it was his only chance.

Noir flattened himself against the floor, bracing as he activated his ferrionics, charging his body to full capacity while the thrusters rumbled to life. Humar slammed his palm against the control panel, and the engines howled—an unholy roar of raw energy surging through the ship's core. A violent detonation followed—not an explosion of destruction, but a rupture of force, an unrestrained blast that propelled the ship forward, clawing against the neutron star's grip.

Pinned to the floor, Noir's body endured the merciless onslaught of acceleration. His muscles convulsed under the strain, his vision flickered, and a red haze bled into his peripheral sight. His heart pounded sluggishly, suffocated by the oppressive force. The metallic taste of blood flooded his mouth as capillaries ruptured from the sheer pressure, his eardrums assaulted by the ship's relentless vibrations. It felt as if his very cells were being stretched, shredded, and reassembled in real-time, his existence reduced to raw agony.

Through the suffocating red fog, he barely registered the screams of the crew—howls of agony wrenched from lungs collapsing under the relentless force. Somewhere, a voice choked, a body convulsed violently, thrashing in its final death throes. Then, silence. Noir knew the void had claimed another.

His mind teetered on the precipice of oblivion, the pain eclipsing anything he had ever endured. But he refused to let go. He clung to consciousness through sheer force of will, his resolve forged in the singular purpose of protecting Saffron—of fighting for the last shred of her humanity.

Suddenly, amid the tumult and agony, a voice broke through the fading edges of his consciousness, cutting through the suffocating haze like a lifeline cast into the void.

"Noir."

The voice was soft but insistent, anchoring him when everything else threatened to collapse. A flicker of recognition ignited in the depths of his mind, a small ember against the encroaching darkness. Noir gritted his teeth, forcing his body to hold on, willing his mind to stay sharp.

But as he lay there, barely tethered to reality, a grim thought slithered into his mind—one he hadn't dared to confront until now.

He had willingly damned himself, the crew, and his own sanity for the sake of a girl he barely knew. A girl who had become something more than just a passenger. A fragile piece of light he had sworn to protect, no matter the cost.

Was it worth it? The lives lost, the sacrifice of his own humanity, all to shield her from the same abyss that now clawed at his soul? The question curled around him like a shadow, tightening its grip.

Noir's breath was ragged, every gasp a battle against the crushing weight pressing down on him. His heart pounded in defiance, each beat a stubborn refusal to let go. His fingers trembled, slick with sweat and blood, but his resolve held fast.

He would die a thousand deaths before surrendering her innocence to monsters like Humar.

The ship groaned under the strain, its very structure protesting against the merciless pull of the neutron star. Every system strained, on the brink of collapse, mirroring the state of the man who refused to yield.

Darkness swirled at the edges of his vision, memories fracturing like shattered glass, slipping beyond his grasp. Who is speaking to me?

He fought to open his eyes, struggling against the unbearable weight of his failing body. The pull was relentless, dragging him down.

Then, the voice came again—steady, urgent.

"Noir. You cannot lose consciousness. You must stay awake. No matter what."

The voice teased the edges of his awareness, familiar yet just beyond reach. A thin spark of recognition stirred, but he remained trapped in darkness, sightless and bound.

"Noir. Open your eyes."

He fought against the suffocating pull, and for a brief moment, he forced his eyelids to part—just a sliver. Above him, Elise Martin leaned close, her normally composed expression marked with something rare. Pain. An ache that made no sense.

She was a hologram, a projection of memory rendered in light and code. Elise should have been untouched by frailty, incapable of human suffering.

"If I were real—if I had a body instead of photons and data—I would cradle you in my arms," she murmured, her voice edged with uncharacteristic softness. "But I cannot. You must wake up, Noir. Somehow, you must. If you want to save Saffron, the ship, and everyone still sleeping within its walls… you *must* wake up."

A groan tore from his throat, every syllable a war against the weight pressing down on him. *"I… can't. I can't."*

Elise's image flickered as she leaned closer, her words piercing through the numbness creeping through his mind.

"You *have* to! Now, get up! Humar and his lackeys are unconscious—but it won't last. You have one chance."

Noir's breath hitched. His eyes, half-lidded and unfocused, barely held onto her face. *"What… do you want me to do?"*

"Didn't you bring the gas mask?" Her voice was sharp, a knife slicing through the fog threatening to pull him under.

He struggled to remember. A distant, slippery thought surfaced. "Yes… I did."

"Then put it on, Noir. Switch it to concentrated oxygen. You need your strength."

With an inhuman effort, Noir lifted a trembling hand, fingers fumbling for the mask at his side. He adjusted the dial with unsteady precision. A soft hiss filled the air, and as he inhaled, a surge of crisp, oxygen-rich air flooded his lungs. It burned—stinging like ice in his chest—before spreading like fire, igniting every sluggish cell in his body.

A faint metallic tang coated his senses. His pulse pounded against his ribs. The fog in his mind began to thin, peeling away layer by layer.

Elise's face softened, her features easing into something almost like relief. "Good. Now, go to Humar. Set the mask to concentrated anesthetic. Ensure he never wakes up."

"Noir," she pressed, her voice an unyielding force against his fractured resolve, "if you don't do this now—if you *fail*—then everything we've fought for, everything we've sacrificed for Saffron, for this ship… will be lost."

Noir groaned as he rolled onto his chest, the rough floor scraping his cheek. Every inch of his body screamed in protest, pain lacing through his muscles as he dragged himself forward, inch by agonizing inch, toward the sleeping animal. The ground beneath him felt like sandpaper, biting into his palms with each movement, raw and unrelenting. Elise's eyes followed him, steady and unreadable, though the faintest glimmer of sadness softened her usually unflinching gaze.

With painstaking effort, Noir finally reached Darin and Fein, securing the masks over their faces, watching as they inhaled the anesthetic gas in slow, fragile breaths. He listened to each intake, rhythmic and deep, and with every exhale, a grim satisfaction settled in his chest.

Then, he turned to Humar.

The warlord lay motionless, his massive form eerily still. Noir carefully adjusted the mask, lowering it toward Humar's face—when suddenly, a steel grip locked around his wrist. Cold fingers, impossibly strong, dug into his skin.

Noir's pulse slammed against his ribs as Humar's eyes flicked open, gleaming with an unnatural light. His lips parted, and a voice that was not his own spilled into the silence, cold and mechanical.

"Who are you? What are you doing?"

Noir swallowed hard, forcing down the panic that threatened to claw its way up his throat. The voice was monotone, soulless—Humar's cyber-mind had awakened. A thousand calculations raced through Noir's mind, and he forced a mask of calm over his face, hoping to outmaneuver the machine.

"I am Noir. The captain of the Wayfarer," he answered, keeping his tone steady, smooth, controlled.

The cyber-mind's gaze locked onto him, unblinking. *"What are you doing with the gas mask?"*

"Administering anesthetic to all passengers," Noir replied, his fingers flexing slightly, tense with unspoken urgency. "It's protocol during high-speed acceleration."

"Why?"

The relentless questioning made his nerves fray at the edges. "So no one… takes harmful actions in response to the acceleration."

A long silence. The cyber-mind's mechanical eyes bore into him, dissecting his every word, every microexpression. Then, the cold voice came again.

"Why aren't you administering it to yourself?"

Noir's heartbeat stuttered. A fine tremor crept into his voice. "I will," he managed, his words as brittle as shattered glass.

"Why haven't you?"

The grip tightened, steel fingers pressing down, threatening to crush bone. Noir barely suppressed a wince. He could feel it—this thing, this intelligence, stripping him down layer by layer, searching for deception, waiting for weakness. Then came the sound. A mechanical whirr, the quiet, deliberate clicking of hidden machinery.

Humar's arm shifted. A sleek, gunmetal extension unfolded from his fingertip. The barrel glowed faintly, humming with charge.

And it was aimed directly at Noir's forehead.

Noir's mind raced, desperate, forcing his sluggish thoughts into coherence. "Because I'm only sedating those who cannot sedate themselves."

A long, agonizing silence stretched between them as the cyber-mind processed his words. Its glowing eyes narrowed into cold, calculating slits, flickering with hesitation. Then—without warning—Humar's grip slackened, his massive hand falling limp. A violent shudder wracked his frame. Noir held his breath, watching as the cyber-mind's connection faltered, its logic caught in an unsolvable loop.

Elise's voice crackled through the comm, relief laced in her words. "Not only did you put him to sleep, Noir, but you've also created a paradox his limited processing can't handle."

Noir barely heard her. His body was shutting down, his limbs leaden, his vision tunneling. He clenched his jaw, forcing himself to focus. "Then let's finish it."

Dragging himself forward in an agonizing crawl, he reached the control panel. His fingers, slick with sweat and blood, closed around the exposed wires. For Saffron. For the Wayfarer. He had to endure. With a ragged breath, he yanked two wires free, then turned back toward Humar's convulsing form.

"Eni," he rasped, his voice barely more than a breath. *"It's now or never."*

Without hesitation, Eni complied. A surge of electricity tore through Humar's body. Sparks erupted in bursts of violent green, the acrid scent of burnt flesh mixing with the sharp tang of fried circuitry. Humar spasmed violently, his eyes bulging, a guttural noise escaping his throat. Smoke seeped from his nostrils and ears, curling upward in thin, ghostly wisps.

With a sickening crunch, something shattered inside him. Tiny gears and metallic shards splintered from his face, cascading to the floor like broken teeth.

Noir clenched his jaw, bile rising in his throat. He had seen death before, had dealt it more times than he cared to count. But this—this was something else. Humar's body stilled. Completely. The unnatural stillness of a machine that had been forcibly silenced.

The quiet was deafening.

Elise's voice finally broke it, her usual composed tone tinged with something almost… human. *"It's over, Noir."* A pause. *"He's… neutralized. For now."*

Noir barely registered her words. His body was giving out, collapsing under exhaustion's weight. He exhaled a shaky breath and let himself sink onto the cold metal floor. His heartbeat slowed, his limbs refusing to move.

"Can I sleep now, Elise?" he murmured, relief threading through the fatigue.

He didn't hear her answer. Her steady, kind face was the last thing he saw before the blackness swallowed him whole.

CHAPTER 9

At The End of The Night

Noir pressed the release option on the medical panel beside Saffron's bed. A soft chime echoed in the quiet room as the restraints unlocked, freeing her pale limbs. With another command, the panel hummed faintly, dispersing the last traces of anesthetic from her system. He didn't take his eyes off her. She lay still, her face softened in the calm of sleep, strands of silvery hair framing features too pure, too unguarded for the horrors she had endured.

She was safe now. Humar would never touch her again.

Minutes passed. A subtle warmth returned to her cheeks, the faint emerald glow beneath her skin pulsing with the slow rhythm of reawakening. Her fingers twitched. Her eyelids fluttered. Then, her head turned with a soft groan, her face contorted by fragments of memories—not dreams.

Noir leaned down, clasping her hand, grounding her.

"Saffron," he whispered. "Open your eyes. I'm here."

Her eyes snapped open, wide, wild. Fear swam in their depths—not the startled kind, but the kind that lingers, the kind that haunts. "Where am I?" she gasped, her voice fragile, raw. "What happened to me?"

Noir's grip tightened, his thumb brushing slow, deliberate strokes over her knuckles. "Nothing happened to you, Saffron. You're still you. You're safe now." His voice was low, steady—a tether pulling her back from the void.

But her breath hitched. "What about Humar Danjon?" she whispered, the name itself like poison on her tongue.

The corner of Noir's mouth twitched in something that wasn't quite a smile, wasn't quite amusement. "You'll never need to worry about him again, Saffron. He's... harmless now."

Her voice trembled, threaded with disbelief. "Where is he?"

He held her gaze, searching for the strength he knew was there. "Come with me, Saffron. You'll see."

But the mere suggestion sent her recoiling. She gripped him tightly, clinging as though letting go meant slipping into oblivion. "No, please! I don't want to see him—I'm afraid," she admitted, her voice breaking as she buried her face into his arm.

"It's all right," Noir murmured, running a hand through her silken hair. *But I think it might help. You'll see that the fear you feel—it has no place here anymore. Not when Humar's own strength has betrayed him.*"

Slowly, his words settled into her. With a hesitant nod, Saffron slipped off the bed. Noir stayed close, his arm a steady presence around her as they moved toward the control room. The air carried a metallic tang of blood, undercut by the acrid stench of burnt machine oil.

Inside, Noir's prisoners—Darin and Fein—slumped in their seats, wrists and ankles bound with unyielding restraints. Darin's bleary eyes fluttered open, unfocused, confusion flickering across his features before melting into something pitiful, almost childlike.

"Captain... please. My nose—it itches," he pleaded, his voice a broken mockery of civility.

Noir regarded him with reluctant pity. He knew all too well what Humar had reduced him to—once an officer of dignity, now a hollowed-out fragment of a man, his mind irreparably altered.

He shook his head. "I can't risk it, Darin. I wish I could say you understand, but Humar's tampering... it's severed the parts of you that might grasp that." His voice was low, edged with something close to sorrow.

Beside him, Fein nodded absently, his gaze vacant. *"We would never hurt you, sir."*

Noir exhaled a weary sigh, rubbing the bridge of his nose. *"Patience, men. I'll see that you're taken care of soon."* But deep down, he knew the truth—they were already lost, fractured echoes of who they had once been.

He turned toward the far corner of the room. There, bound to thick heat-conducting tubes, lay Humar.

The terrifying fusion of man and machine, the creature who had once commanded fear across the cosmos, now looked like the shattered wreckage of a nightmare.

Saffron gasped. Her fingers dug into Noir's arm, nails pressing deep, her entire body trembling against his. He welcomed the pain. It meant she was here. That she was real. That she could still feel.

"Humar is no longer the monster you knew," Noir said softly. "He's barely even a man."

But Saffron's face twisted in revulsion, her breath coming in short, uneven bursts. *"Look at him,"* she whispered, her voice breaking. *"He's... he's repulsive."*

She wasn't wrong.

Humar's left eye dangled precariously, held in place only by the frayed strands of optic nerves. His face was a grotesque fusion of exposed machine parts and decaying flesh, a grim testament to the monster he had become. A thick, noxious mixture of blood and lubricant seeped from his wounds, trailing down his cheek in slow, viscous drips, pooling into a dark, stagnant puddle at his feet.

He was no longer the formidable cyborg who had once commanded fear. Now, he was nothing more than the wreckage of his own arrogance.

Humar's remaining eye flickered weakly, locking onto Noir's with something that almost resembled recognition. His breath was ragged, every syllable escaping his lips like rusted metal grinding against stone.

"Noir..." he rasped, his voice barely more than static. *"Kill me. End this."*

Noir's expression remained cold, unyielding. *"If I wanted you dead, I would've left you on that damned moon, left you to whatever fate was waiting."*

Humar's shattered face twisted with desperation, his jaw clenching. "You think... you're sparing me?" His mangled throat convulsed as he forced out another breath. "Then get a weapon and finish it."

The words carried the weight of irreversible loss, spoken by a man who had long since ceased to exist.

Saffron flinched, her breath hitching as a shudder ran through her. She turned her face away, pressing against Noir's chest, unwilling—unable—to look at the man who had nearly stolen her will, her very sense of self. Noir held her close, but his gaze never left Humar.

"I'm not giving you that freedom," Noir replied, his voice devoid of sympathy. "Our civilization has medical advancements beyond your comprehension. They'll repair you, rebuild whatever's left of that damaged mind of yours. They'll give you back your humanity."

Humar's remaining eye darkened, his lips curling into something between a grimace and a smirk. *"Then that person won't be me."* His voice was thick with contempt, edged with something far more damning—fear. *"I'll be someone else."*

Noir hesitated.

For the first time, the certainty in his resolve wavered. The raw truth in Humar's words cut deeper than he had expected, striking at something he wasn't prepared to confront.

He glanced at Saffron, still curled into him, her breaths quick and shallow. She was safe. Humar was broken. And yet, the weight of his decision settled heavily on him.

In that stillness, Noir understood the cost of his own mercy. A mercy that would erase Humar's flaws—but also his identity.

* * *

It took a great while for Noir and Saffron to load Humar and his altered followers, Darin and Fein, into their cryo capsules. For Darin and Fein, the procedure was met with an eerie ease; both men surrendered to the coming sleep with a hollow acceptance, their eyes glazed over, nearly vacant. But Humar was a different story entirely.

As the lid descended over his capsule, his pleas began—ragged, desperate, each word jagged with fear. *"Kill me. Kill me, damn you— don't freeze me!"* His voice fractured into strangled tones, his breath fogging against the cryo-glass as he thrashed against his restraints. "Noir! You don't understand! You can't leave me like this—Noir!"

But the chamber sealed with a final hiss, drowning his voice in sterile silence.

Through the misted glass, Humar's face became a ghost of the man he once was—twisted in terror, eyes wild with a realization far too late. He had not understood, not until now. Not until he saw his fate mirrored back at him. Noir watched without expression. Humar was already dead in every way that mattered, and his struggle meant nothing.

Once the villains were locked away in their metal tombs, Noir exhaled deeply, shifting his focus to the damage the Wayfarer had sustained.

The ship had barely survived the neutron star's gravitational snare. The primary control module was in ruins, the worst-hit part of the ship, its shattered wiring sparking weakly like the last flickers of a dying pulse. The emergency backup module hung on by a thread, its flickering lights casting sporadic bursts of dim illumination as if uncertain of its own survival. Heat transfer pipes had twisted and fractured under the strain, their jagged edges sharp from the force of their rupture.

And then there were the micro-fractures.

Thin, web-like fissures had spread across the hull, leaking precious air with a nearly imperceptible hiss—a whispered countdown to disaster. Noir had been forced to seal off entire sections of the ship, confining the usable space to what little remained undamaged.

The communications module was barely functional, its last distress signal to the Galactic Operations Center lost hours ago. If he couldn't reestablish contact soon, they'd be presumed dead—another ghost swallowed by the star.

In the dim corridors of the Wayfarer, Noir glanced over at Saffron. She stood alert, her stance firm, tension creasing her brow.

He had asked her—twice, then a third time—to return to cryosleep, to rest while he handled the repairs.

But she refused.

"I'm staying awake," she had declared, arms crossed, her voice steady with quiet defiance. *"You need another set of hands, and I know my way around a repair wrench."*

Noir could have pressed the issue, reminded her that protocol dictated otherwise. Keeping her awake was not only unconventional—it was a breach of regulation. But he didn't argue further.

Truth be told, he was relieved.

There was something grounding about her presence—a contrast to the ship's ominous groans and metallic creaks. Her voice cut through the tense quiet, a reminder that amidst the ruin, he was not alone.

Together, they worked through the ship's damaged innards. And, to his surprise, she wasn't unskilled—far from it. Back on her home planet, she had run a modest but respected hover-car repair shop, giving her a natural dexterity and a familiarity with tools that put his mind slightly at ease. Saffron deftly guided Eni, the ship's AI, through minor repairs, issuing commands with a confidence he hadn't expected. Noir caught himself watching her more than once, a grudging admiration growing as she navigated the damaged corridors, unshaken by the hostile environment they were trying to salvage.

Later, with Humar and his men sealed away and Saffron finally resting, Noir wandered the ship alone, sifting through the wreckage they were left to repair. He called out softly, "Eni? You there?"

The AI responded almost immediately, its tone crisp yet composed. "Yes, Captain Noir."

Noir leaned against the wall, surveying the dim-lit expanse of circuitry and ruined panels. "The ship's gutted. Feels like we're drifting through our own wreckage. It's hostile in here."

"I concur," Eni replied, a trace of artificial humor slipping into its otherwise neutral tone.

He exhaled, absorbing the weight of their predicament. *"What's priority one? Where do I even start?"*

Eni hesitated for a millisecond, a flicker of code processing. "The communication module, Captain. It has been offline since the first impact. If it is not restored soon, the Galactic Operations Center will assume we were lost to the star."

"Got it," Noir replied, bracing himself—only for Eni to interrupt.

"You cannot begin there, Captain. The communication module requires a functional main control unit. The main control, however, cannot be repaired until the hull's micro-fractures are sealed to prevent structural breach."

Noir huffed a quiet laugh, exhausted but appreciating the logic. *"Of course. No shortcuts. All right, release the engineer bots. I'll get started. Saffron said she'd help."*

The void enveloped Noir and Saffron as they floated alongside the *Wayfarer*—a slumbering giant riddled with jagged, hairline fractures, scars carved by the neutron star's merciless pull. They were clad in sleek, hyper-maneuverable suits, each emitting faint blue-white light trails as they moved with measured precision.

Eni had dispatched twelve engineer bots, six for each of them. The small machines buzzed and clicked like a mechanical swarm, responding to commands as they glided over the hull. Each crack felt like an open wound to Noir, each scar a battle survived. The bots emitted a focused laser that fused the fractures with reinforced metal alloys, the heat flaring bright red before fading into smooth, unblemished plating. Noir observed, the acrid tang of scorched metal seeping through his suit's air supply.

Saffron's voice broke the silence, warm yet uncertain. "I'm sorry I can't be of much use," she murmured. *All I know are hover-cars and bikes. Fixing a beast like the Wayfarer... it's like standing in a forge of the gods. I just don't compare.* Her voice trailed off.

Noir glanced at her as his bot completed its pass over a fracture, a small smile tugging at his lips. "Not true at all, Saffron," he replied. "You're guiding the bots perfectly, and that's keeping us alive right now. Besides," he added, his voice softening, *your presence here means more to me than you could know.*

She didn't answer, but in the brief pause, he noticed her visor dip slightly, as if she had turned away to hide her face. Though separated by space, he could tell she was blushing—a small touch of warmth against the cold void.

Noir's chest tightened. "You've had to endure so much as a passenger here, Saffron," he continued, his voice growing solemn. *Please accept my apologies as captain. If you'd like, I can even file an official apology…*

A laugh crackled through the comm channel—light, unexpected. It was like creek water rushing over smooth stones, free and musical, cutting through the weight of their situation. "Oh, please," she chuckled. *Don't give me an official apology. How unfair would that* be? You have all this authority as captain, but I can't file an official thank-you for saving my life!"

Noir's own chuckle joined hers. He realized why he had broken protocol and let her stay awake—her presence softened the lonely, steely silence of space. "To be fair, both of us were lucky just to survive," he admitted, his tone sobering. *"The odds weren't exactly in our favor."* He hesitated, a wistful smile crossing his lips. *"I had brought a bonsai tree from Lightlore for my mother. She always wanted one. By now, it should've blossomed."*

Saffron nodded, an understanding glimmer in her eyes. "We were fortunate," she murmured, *"because you were our captain. Without you, we wouldn't be here."*

Noir's breath caught at the quiet sincerity in her words, but before he could respond, she activated her jetpack, gliding toward him in a smooth, deliberate motion. She stopped just in front of him, close enough that he could see her features clearly through her visor. Slowly, she reached out, her gloved hands meeting his. A faint tremor passed through their gloves at the contact—warmth against the unyielding cold of space. Her eyes, steady and unflinching, met his.

"I'm grateful to you, Noir," she said softly, her voice carrying a weight that went beyond mere words. *"For more than saving my life. You taught me something I didn't expect to find out here—that we have to hold onto our humanity, even when it's hard, even when it costs us everything."*

A nervous laugh escaped him, awkward and honest. *"Ah, you can thank my mother for that,"* he replied. *"She's always been more concerned about my 'humanity' than intellect or strength. She didn't even genetically modify me— wanted me born naturally, with all the messiness that entails. Said she couldn't bear the thought of altering what makes us human."*

Saffron's smile was rare, like a pale moon breaking through an endless night. *"Your mother sounds like an incredible woman, Noir. What better gift could she give you than your humanity?"*

Noir shrugged, feeling the faint pull of melancholy in her words. "It doesn't always feel like an asset, especially out here."

Saffron's voice lowered. "Where is she now?"

"Close to our destination," he answered, his voice softening. *"That's part of why I took this job—to see her again. I was going to surprise her with the good luck bonsai tree."*

A silence settled between them, weighted with unspoken thoughts. When Saffron finally spoke, her voice was barely more than a whisper. "You're lucky, Noir.

Someone dear to you is waiting. I… don't have anyone left."

For a fleeting moment, Noir thought he caught something in her gaze—expectation, maybe, or a longing that ran deeper than words.

I'm here, Saffron. I'll be here for you.

The thought pressed against his mind, struggling to break free, but he couldn't voice it.

Instead, he managed a quiet, *"You'll find someone, Saffron. I know you will."*

She looked at him, and something flickered in her eyes—a sadness, layered with an unreadable depth that left him unsettled. Then, without a word, she moved back, releasing his hands and returning to the bots. But her silence lingered.

For reasons he couldn't explain, Noir's chest tightened, an ache pressing against his ribs. It was a hollow, twisting kind of pain, leaving him feeling strangely exposed. He watched her work, and in that silence, he felt the distance between them deepen, as if it was more than just the empty space around them.

* * *

Noir and Saffron pressed on, swallowed by the relentless cycle of repairs. Hours blurred together until their meticulous hands sealed the last hairline fracture on the Wayfarer's hull. When they finally reentered the ship, they moved like the walking dead—feet dragging under the weight of exhaustion, arms barely responding as they struggled to lift their helmets and unlatch their gloves. Every muscle screamed in protest, their bodies betraying them. Speech was a luxury they couldn't afford; all they managed were faint nods before staggering toward their quarters.

In his cabin, Noir stopped short, stunned to see Elise Martin. Her holographic form bathed the room in a pale-blue glow, the soft light tempering the usual precision of her presence.

"Elise…" he managed, barely standing.

She smiled, a faint, almost sorrowful curve of her lips. "I came to say farewell, Noir."

A chill slid down his spine at her words. "Farewell?"

Elise's gaze held steady, but there was a distant kind of pride in it. "You handled this ordeal admirably. You don't need me anymore."

"No." Noir shook his head, though even the motion felt like too much effort. *"You don't understand how much I still need you. I wouldn't have made it without your guidance."*

Elise's laughter was soft, distant, like the chime of bells carried on a dying breeze. *"You admire me too much, Noir. Survival isn't about needing someone else—it's about believing you have what it takes, even when you think you don't. And you did that."*

He let out a breath, feeling something small but real take root in his chest. "I promise I'll try."

Stepping closer, Elise's expression turned unexpectedly tender, her eyes flickering with an intensity she rarely showed. *"If only I could touch your face, to reassure you.*" She exhaled softly, eyes glistening. "But… you know what's real, Noir. And those who are real should never deceive themselves."

Noir hesitated, absorbing her words, even as their meaning eluded him. Her hologram flickered, the projection wavering like a ghost caught between dimensions.

"I'll remember you, Elise," he whispered.

Elise's face softened further, shadowed with something between gratitude and farewell. *"I wish you luck, Noir. And when you see her, give your mother my regards. She's given the galaxy a gift."*

Then, she faded from his quarters, her absence leaving behind a cavernous silence that twisted deep in his chest.

With a heavy heart and renewed resolve, Noir activated the ship's comm module, transmitting a full report to the Galactic Operations Center, slipping in a humble yet determined request to locate his mother. As he waited, he refocused on his work with Saffron, burying himself in tasks that demanded precision—anything to temper the emotions Elise's final words had stirred.

In the days that followed, Noir and Saffron settled into an efficient rhythm, repairs shifting from frantic necessity to something almost companionable. As if by unspoken agreement, they lingered over mealtimes, laughing at small absurdities, savoring a fleeting but welcome calm.

One evening, after an exhausting shift, they finally took a breather, sitting across from each other in the mess hall as Eni, the ship's AI, had outdone herself with a hot, fragrant meal. Steam curled from their bowls, carrying the rich, savory scent of synthesized spices and herbs—a faint attempt at mimicking the earthy aroma of a garden. Noir took the first sip, the broth sliding down like a balm, though his muscles protested the simple act of lifting the spoon.

Their conversation drifted into lighter territory, swapping stories of past adventures and near disasters, their laughter breaking through the ship's metallic cold. Saffron's laugh carried a warmth that softened the sterile air of the *Wayfarer,* and Noir found himself marveling at how her presence reshaped the space around them.

As the meal wound down, something shifted between them—an invisible gravity that pulled their words into quiet. Noir could feel her presence sharpening, her gaze steady, carrying a soft spark that made his pulse stutter. They leaned in, their faces mere inches apart, her breath warm and subtly sweet from the meal, mingling with his in the narrow space between them.

For a moment, the universe—the daunting infinity beyond the ship's walls—receded, leaving only this sliver of fragile, exquisite clarity between them. Noir hesitated, Elise's words ghosting through his mind: *Do not deceive yourself.* He exhaled, letting the fear slip from his heart.

Saffron's tentacles brushed against his hands, hesitant yet certain, her eyes wide with something close to wonder—an innocent surprise, as if she hadn't expected to be here, yet couldn't imagine being anywhere else.

Noir's breath caught. In this improbable, weightless moment, he felt something stir—something he had long feared to hope for, something infused with her warmth. A faint tremor ran through his fingers as he clasped her tentacles, and their laughter faded into a serene, knowing silence.

"What are you waiting for?" Saffron whispered.

Noir's eyebrows lifted slightly, a smile tugging at his lips at the longing in her gaze. He tilted her chin up, then brushed his lips softly against hers.

A shiver passed through her at his touch.

Noir pulled back, his voice laced with quiet happiness. *"I've wanted to kiss you for a long time, Saffron—"*

He never finished the sentence. She gripped the fabric of his suit and pulled him closer. Noir inhaled sharply, warmth rushing through him at the intensity in her eyes. He couldn't hold back any longer. Threading his fingers through her thick, silken hair, he pressed his mouth to hers, deepening the kiss as she met him with equal urgency.

Her scent, a delicate mix of something floral with a faint hint of mint, filled his senses. He slid his hands to her waist, pulling her flush against him. A tremor ran through him as she melted into him, the space between them disappearing. Their lips parted, tongues meeting in slow, heated strokes.

They rose from their chairs in unspoken agreement, their hands exploring, learning. Noir backed her against the wall, his thigh slipping between hers, eliciting a quiet gasp from her. Saffron's six arms wrapped around him, anchoring him against her, her skin warm even through the fabric of his uniform. Noir groaned softly as she pressed into him, the heat of her body sending a pulse of desire through his veins. Saffron whimpered as his lips trailed down her neck, leaving a path of heat in their wake. "Kiss me," she murmured, her voice barely a breath.

He obeyed, capturing her mouth once more, his deep kiss unraveling something inside her. She pulled him closer with two of her tentacles, her breathing turning shallow, her body instinctively molding against his. Their movements grew hungrier, lips and tongues seeking, devouring.

Noir felt himself sinking into her, into the intoxicating mix of warmth and sensation, lost in the gravity of this moment.

Saffron whispered into his ear, her breath warm against his skin. "I think I'm falling for you, Noir."

Noir's gaze held hers, steady and intense. *Did I ever tell you how beautiful you are?"*

Their eyes remained locked as they shed their layers, hands moving with slow, deliberate intent, unfastening clasps and peeling away the barriers between them.

Noir pressed against her, feeling the heat of her body, the way she trembled beneath him. Then, with a slow, measured push, he entered her. Saffron gasped, her fingers tightening around his arms.

"I'm sorry," Noir murmured, his voice rough, uncertain.

Saffron exhaled shakily, her chest rising against his. "It's okay. I'm okay," she reassured him between ragged breaths. "Keep going."

She widened her hips, anchoring herself against him, gripping his shoulders for leverage. Noir moved, each thrust deeper, more certain. Saffron wrapped her legs around his waist, locking her ankles behind his back as his movements intensified. The friction sent shivers through her, gasps escaping her throat, her nails digging into his skin.

"Fuck," Noir groaned, pressing his forehead against hers. "You're incredible."

Tension coiled between them, tightening like a drawn bowstring as Noir quickened his rhythm. Saffron met him, her body moving in sync with his, her breath coming in quick, heated bursts. A spark of wild urgency flared within her, and she bit his neck—not hard enough to hurt, but enough to mark him, to make him hers.

Noir growled, gripping her tighter, his body moving with a force as relentless as a ship surging through hyperspace. Saffron clung to him, her arms tightening, her fingers pressing into his back as the sensations overwhelmed her. She met his eyes, and for a moment, it was as if everything outside this moment ceased to exist—the vast emptiness of space, the remnants of war and survival.

Noir plunged deeper, driving her toward the edge. Her entire body tensed, her back arching as waves of pleasure surged through her, white-hot and electric. She cried out as the release tore through her, her body shuddering in his hold.

Noir's rhythm faltered, his breath coming in ragged gasps. He groaned, low and guttural, before stilling with a final, deep thrust. His muscles tensed, a sharp exhale escaping him as he surrendered to the sensation.

For a moment, neither of them moved. The only sound was the quiet hum of the ship around them, the air thick with warmth and shared breath.

Noir exhaled, lowering himself onto the large adjacent couch, bringing her with him. He lay over her, his face buried in her hair, inhaling her scent as he listened to the wild rhythm of their heart-beats, hers mirroring his— quick, frantic, alive.

Saffron's tentacles wrapped around him, curling around his shoulders, his back, his neck, holding him close. She wanted to keep him there, tethered to her, just a little longer.

After a while, Noir shifted, lifting his head, propping himself up on one arm. His lips quirked into a small, playful smile as he traced a gentle kiss along her cheek, then her temple, then the corner of her eye.

Saffron sighed softly, her fingers brushing against his jaw, anchoring herself in the quiet afterglow.

Saffron smiled, a radiant warmth blooming in her chest. Her voice was soft, teasing. "That was amazing. Can we do that again?"

Noir chuckled, the sound low and affectionate. He brushed a slow, lingering kiss against her lips before murmuring, "At this rate, we'll never get the ship fixed."

* * *

As the days passed, Noir and Saffron found themselves stealing glances, slipping away from the relentless routine to share fleeting moments of pleasure and closeness. Those stolen minutes felt like rare starlight piercing the void, a fragile reprieve from the weight of survival. With the *Wayfarer* in disrepair, the steady hum of machines and the whir of repair drones became the backdrop to their whispered conversations and shared touches. Amid the tang of ozone—the charged scent of exposed circuitry each moment together felt delicate, fleeting, irreplaceable.

Restoring the *Wayfarer* wasn't grueling labor, but it was long, exhaustive work. Noir focused first on recalibrating the ship's intricate energy conduction systems. Days blurred together as he realigned pathways, ran diagnostics, and wrestled with tangled conduits, the acrid scent of heated metal clinging to the air like burnt dust. His body ached from the strain, his mind dulled by repetition, but in the periphery of his vision, Saffron moved—her sixarmed form a graceful contrast to the mechanical disarray.

Even as he fought with ruptured cooling pipes and misaligned circuits, the sight of her stirred something deep within him, a hunger that had nothing to do with exhaustion.

After restoring the electrical conduits, Noir turned his attention to the ship's heat distribution systems. The specialized super-alloy tubes, twisted and contorted from past impacts, were now slick with leaking coolant. He cleaned each area meticulously, the frigid liquid leaving a metallic tang in the air, chilling his fingertips as he wiped it away. Repairing the damaged tubing felt like suturing open wounds, but he pressed on, forcing himself to double-check every connection, every weld. Once the repairs were complete, he cycled the cooling fluid through the main pump, listening as the low whir and rhythmic rumble signaled the system coming back to life.

Despite his efforts, exhaustion gnawed at him, but he pushed forward, drawing what strength he could from the brief moments of solace he shared with Saffron.

Time became fluid, slipping past them as they lost themselves in the enormity of the task. They drove each other to keep going, to see the work through, leaning on each other like survivors clinging to the last embers of warmth. Eni's calm, methodical voice was a constant, a steady pulse guiding them through the monotony and strain.

One evening, as Saffron rested in Noir's quarters now the place she instinctively sought for sleep—Eni's alert cut through the quiet.

"Captain Noir, the Wayfarer has reestablished a link with Galactic Operations."

Noir froze, a tremor of hope breaking through his fatigue. "Finally," he muttered, setting his tools aside and making his way to the control room. He sank into the captain's chair, anticipation and relief settling in his chest like a weight he hadn't realized he was carrying.

The monitor flickered, revealing the Galactic Operations board of supervisors, their faces lined with tension. The debate was already in full force.

"Damn the Lightlore branch," one of them barked. "What were they thinking, loading a criminal like Humar Danjon onto the Wayfarer without a full security protocol?"

Noir's eyes narrowed, his interest waning as the debates raged on, but he endured it, waiting for the critical piece of information he had been hoping for.

Other officials, less heated, commended him for maneuvering the *Wayfarer* out of the neutron star's deadly grasp and for encountering a rare cosmic life form. Their praise was an afterthought, a distant murmur in the back of his mind as he watched the screen with a steady, unyielding gaze.

At last, one of the officials addressed Noir's request—a desperate plea for any information about his mother's whereabouts.

"We've located her," the man said.

Noir's heart surged with hope, only to falter at the solemn expression on the man's face.

The screen flickered, shifting to a middle-aged man with weary eyes, his voice thick with regret.

"Captain Noir," he began softly, "your mother… she was informed that the *Wayfarer* had been lost near the neutron star." He hesitated, his eyes glistening, as if struggling to shape the words. "She waited for updates, hoping against all odds. But as the days passed, that hope began to fade."

Noir's hands clenched the edges of his chair, his knuckles turning white.

"One night, under a full moon, she walked into the ocean. We found her body washed ashore with a note." The official's voice wavered. "I'm so very sorry, Captain."

The screen went dark, leaving Noir in stunned silence, staring at the empty console. The vast control room, once alive with humming panels and flickering readouts, now felt like an abyss. The soft glow of the nebula beyond the viewport cast shifting hues of blue and violet across the walls, a cruel contrast to the hollow stillness consuming him.

His gaze drifted to the small bonsai tree perched on the console—a gift meant for her, its twisted branches stretching skyward, reaching for something no longer within his grasp. It felt meaningless now, a relic of a future that would never be.

Eni's voice broke the silence. "I've received a transmission—a final message from your mother. Would you like to view it?"

Noir barely managed a nod. The hologram flickered to life.

There she was. His mother.

Her raven-black hair drifted in a ghostly breeze, her sapphire eyes reflecting sorrow as vast as the cosmos. Her voice was barely a whisper.

"I wanted to see my son… to hold him one last time."

She paused, her gaze shifting upward, beyond the unseen boundaries of the world she was leaving behind.

"They say we become stars after we die. I hope I will find you, my son, somewhere in that endless night."

Her image wavered, beginning to dissolve into static.

Noir, overwhelmed, lurched forward, his voice breaking as he shouted at the empty space before him.

A voice reached him from behind, soft and full of warmth.

"Noir," Saffron called, stepping into his line of sight, her six arms wrapping around him, drawing him close. "I'm here," she murmured, stroking his face with gentle fingers.

He buried his face against her shoulder, his body trembling as the sobs overtook him.

His voice cracked as he whispered, "Stay with me, Saffron. Don't leave me alone."

She held him tighter, pressing her forehead to his. *"I will never leave you, Noir. Never."*

A soft shadow fell beside them. Noir lifted his gaze to see Great Elise standing there, her hologram flickering slightly, her expression calm yet resolute.

"I felt it wouldn't be right to leave you just yet," she said with a faint smile. "Humans need each other, Noir. Even the strongest of us."

He reached out a hand, his eyes filled with gratitude. "Thank you, Elise. For everything."

Eni's voice chimed softly in the background. *"Commencing deletion of brain mapping."*

Elise gave a final nod, her form wavering before dissolving into the ambient glow of the ship's interface.

Noir closed his eyes, his grip on Saffron tightening as the quiet hum of the *Wayfarer* settled around them.

Soon, the ship's engines rumbled to life once more, their deep, resonant roar filling the silence.

And so the *Wayfarer* carried two lone passengers toward their destination.

Noir and Saffron.

The End